COUSINS

NOT QUITE SISTERS

COUSINS

NOT QUITE SISTERS

Colleen O'Shaughnessy McKenna

AN
APPLE
PAPERBACK

SCHOLASTIC INC.
New York Toronto London Auckland Sydney

ISBN 0-590-49428-7

12 11 10 9 8 7 6 5 4 3 2   3 4 5 6 7 8/9

Printed in the U.S.A.   40

First Scholastic printing, July 1993

COUSINS

NOT QUITE SISTERS

1

"**I** hope Aunt Sharon and Jessica get here soon. I can hardly wait to see them." I tacked another balloon onto the welcome banner I was making. My favorite aunt and my ten-year-old cousin, Jessica, were moving down from Pittsburgh to live in Sweetwater. "Just think, Mom. All my cousins will finally live in Texas. Six cousins and a dozen aunts and uncles."

"I know, Callie. It's going to be wonderful." Mom stepped over my banner. "Since you're the oldest cousin, I'm counting on you to help Jessica feel right at home."

"I know. Don't worry, Mom, Jessica has always fit in just fine," I assured her.

"Things might be a little different this time. Jessica isn't just coming for a visit. Because of the divorce, Sweetwater will be her new home." Mom poured herself another cup of coffee and glanced at the phone. It had to be her fifteenth cup.

"Jessica will love it down here. Anyway, Lind-

1

say and I have already planned so much fun stuff, Jessica won't have time to get homesick." I studied my sign. It was one of my best. "Thanks for letting us have the welcome party here on Saturday, Mom."

"What?" My mother set down her cup and shook her head. "Oh, I forgot about that. Was that for *this* Saturday?"

"Yep. Seven-thirty, on the dot." I could hardly wait to introduce Jessica to all my friends. Jessica was so funny, she would be a big hit.

"*This* Saturday?" my mom repeated again. She didn't sound or look the least bit excited.

"Yes. You said it was all right." I flung back my thick reddish braids and sat up straighter. My mom was acting awfully weird all of a sudden.

"I didn't think you meant *this* Saturday," my mother repeated for the third time. "That's in a few days, Callie."

"I know. Don't worry about a thing, Mom. Jessica has already met some of the kids before, and Lindsay and I are going to do everything. I mean, you can give me some money for the food, but we'll set up, shop, and clean up."

My mother nodded. "I know you'd be a big help, honey, but maybe we're rushing things a little. I mean, Jessica isn't really herself these days. The divorce has been so hard on her."

"That's why she needs a party," I pointed out.

2

"And it will be small, Mom, maybe only ten or twelve kids. Five or six of Lindsay's friends, since Jessica will be starting sixth grade with her, and some of my friends from the seventh grade."

Mom was chewing on her lower lip, the way she does right before she says no to something. "Let me give it a little more thought, honey. Aunt Sharon may not even get here till Thursday."

"That will work out great. Jessica can rest all day Friday and have lots of fun on Saturday." I walked over and wrapped my arm around my mom's neck. "Come *ooooooon*, Mom. You did ask me to cheer Jessica up."

Mom patted my arm and nodded. "I know. But, Jessica misses her father. He left Pittsburgh without even saying good-bye."

What a jerk. I wouldn't miss Uncle Bernie, and I *knew* my parents wouldn't miss Uncle Burn-out, as my dad called him.

"Trust me, Mom. The party is a great idea. Lindsay and I are her favorite cousins, and we know her the best." I went back to work on my banner and added a row of red hearts.

My mother sat up straighter and leaned forward.

"Callie, there are some things you don't know about Jessica."

"What?" I dropped my marker. I had been pals with Jessica since she was a baby. We wrote let-

3

ters, visited on summer vacations, called each other on our birthdays. "Mom, I know Jessica inside and out."

"You're still very young, and can't imagine all the emotional complications and . . ."

"Mom," I groaned. I hate it when Mom tells me that I am too young to understand. She can't see inside my head. I understand lots more than she thinks I do. "I'm emotional, too, Mom. And complicated." I drew in a deep breath and stopped. I could feel my temper heating up. My temper must have been built into my red hair, and it was one trait my mom wasn't thrilled with. "I wish you would trust me about this party, Mom. I *know* what I'm doing. The whole point of a welcome party is to welcome someone right away."

The phone rang and my mom dove for it. This had been going on all weekend. Since Mom usually yells, "Tell them I'm busy!" as soon as the phone rings, I was starting to wonder why her phone calls were suddenly so important. I think she had already talked to every aunt in Texas.

"I'll take the call in the living room."

I got up and leaned against the door, listening. I am not normally a big sneak, but I was dying to find out what was going on. I had the feeling it was an emotional complication.

Even though my mom was trying to keep her voice down low, I could feel the anger. Uncle Bernie must have pulled another fast one.

"Hello, hello!" Lindsay pressed her face against the screen and stuck out her tongue. "I have arrived!"

"And just in time," I whispered. I opened the screen door and pulled her inside.

"Hey, watch the merchandise." Lindsay laughed. "I know you're happy to see me, but calm down."

"My mom is talking to Aunt Sharon," I hissed.

"Great!" Lindsay reached across me and grabbed a banana from the basket. "Are they on their way?"

"No. I mean, I don't know." I pulled her closer to the doorway. "My mom sounds mad."

Lindsay put down the banana. "Well, hey, don't tell her I tried to steal a banana."

"She's mad about Uncle Bernie."

Lindsay rolled her eyes. "Oh, brother, *everyone* is mad about Uncle Bernie. I will be *sooooo* glad when Jessica is down here with us." Lindsay broke into a huge smile. "Guess who said he can come to our party!"

"Scott Randel!" It wasn't too hard to guess. Scott Randel was probably the cutest boy in Texas. Lindsay had been trying to convince him to come to our party for three days.

"Yes!" Lindsay spun around. "He finally said yes. We are so lucky. I mean, this kid doesn't go to just *anyone's* party."

I decided not to ruin her happiness with news

that the party might be postponed. "It will be the social event of the summer," I said, batting my eyes at Lindsay.

"But, of course, Callie, dear. And if young Mr. Randel is coming, I think we should def-i-nitely go with the best caterer in town."

I opened the pantry door and pulled out a bag of chips. "I've already started to shop."

Lindsay and I started to laugh. She is only eleven months younger than I and so much fun. I was going to miss her and her goofy smile once I started junior high next year.

"Jessica will die when she finds out he's coming." Lindsay slid onto the kitchen chair. "He looks fourteen, at least. And he said he'll bring five of his best tapes. I tried to call her last night to give her the good news but Aunt Sharon said she couldn't come to the phone."

"Yeah, I haven't been able to catch her, either."

"I feel sooooo bad for her," said Lindsay. Then she smiled. "Well, with cousins as cool as we are, she'll be feeling better soon."

Mom walked back in the kitchen, her cheeks flushed. She went straight to the coffee pot and filled up her cup. "Good morning, Lindsay. How are you doing, honey?"

"I'm fine, thanks, Aunt Ellie. My mom wants you to call her and let her know when Aunt Sharon's getting in."

My mother nodded. "Aunt Sharon just called. They haven't left yet."

I glanced down at the balloons taped to my welcome banner. They would go limp in the June heat before my cousin ever left Pittsburgh.

"Great," I muttered. I was so disappointed, it was making me mad. "This is the fourth time they've delayed the trip. Maybe Aunt Sharon wants to *stay* in Pittsburgh."

"Trust me, Callie, Aunt Sharon does *not* want to stay in Pittsburgh," my mother said firmly. "Jessica needs more time."

"More time?" I squeaked.

"Time for what?" asked Lindsay. "Her cousins have been waiting for two weeks!"

"Three weeks," I corrected. I walked over and picked up my banner. "And I'm tired of waiting." Patience was not one of my strong suits. "As the oldest cousin, I think it's my job to call Aunt Sharon. I'll tell Jessica she is the guest of honor at our party on Saturday."

"Callie," Mom said, sinking into her chair.

Lindsay slung her arm around my shoulder. "Way to go, Callie. And remind Jessica that Scott Randel is coming to the party on Saturday."

"I know you're disappointed, girls." Mom looked pretty disappointed herself. She started stirring her coffee so fast, a small tornado swirled around inside her cup.

7

Lindsay walked over and picked up the phone. "Go on, Callie. Call her."

"Don't!" Mom stood up and took the phone from Lindsay. "No one should call Jessica right now."

"Why not?" I wanted to know. Somebody had to do something.

"Because," my mother said slowly, "Jessica won't talk to you."

I laughed. "Sure, she will."

My mother shook her head, a few tears washing over her eyes. "No, Callie, she won't. Jessica hasn't said a word to anyone for days."

2

"What do you mean?" I wanted to know. "Is Jessica on some sort of verbal hunger strike?" My cousin Jessica normally talked nonstop. Lindsay had nicknamed her Motor Mouth last Christmas. And whenever I called her long distance, Mom had to set the oven timer for ten minutes so we wouldn't talk for hours.

"It's rather serious," Mom said. "Jessica won't speak."

"Is she in the hospital?" asked Lindsay. "Can they fix her?"

"She's been to a child psychologist, and he said to just give Jessica time to deal with the divorce." Mom ran her fingers through her blonde hair. "I've never even heard of a child going mute, and . . ."

Mute? Boy, even the word sounded serious, like Jessica's voice box had been chopped off. Mute!

The phone rang again and Mom started talking

to another aunt. I grabbed Lindsay's arm and pointed outside.

"I can't believe it," Lindsay said, flopping down on the porch swing. "How can you just stop talking?"

My own mouth felt dry and hollow. Whenever I got mad or worried, I just lost my temper. Then my mom would send me to my room. After ten or twenty minutes, I was back to normal.

But, how long did it take to get back to normal when you were stuck at mute?

Lindsay sighed. "I think the longest I go without talking is the eight hours I'm asleep."

"Trust me, Lindsay, you talk in your sleep."

Lindsay made a face and then laughed. "So maybe I have a lot to say. Hey, Callie, does this mean that Jessica has cracked up? Had some sort of a mental breakdown?"

"No. She'll be okay," I tried to sound like I knew what I was talking about. Truth was, I was getting a little scared myself. I walked back to the screen door and listened. I hoped when my mom got off the phone, she would rush outside to assure us that Jessica was going to be all right.

"Callie," Lindsay said, "people who stop talking can be really weird. I saw this creepy movie last summer about a man who stopped talking after he saw his father shoot his mother in the forehead with a bow and arrow." Lindsay frowned. "Or maybe he saw his mother shoot his father. Anyway, he never spoke till the end of the movie. Then, right before he was sent to the insane asylum, he said good-bye."

"Good, Lindsay. Thanks a lot for making me feel so much better about Jessica with that cheerful bit of information." I hopped up on the railing and shook my finger at her. "That is not going to happen to Jessica. We can find a way to cheer her up."

"I wonder if Uncle Bernie did something to scare her." Lindsay chewed on the end of her ponytail. "Remember two Christmases ago when Uncle Bernie told the whole table that Aunt Sharon was a lousy cook? He said she had a hard time getting water to boil."

"So?" I mean, it isn't nice to rip on someone, but saying someone is a crummy cook isn't as bad as shooting a bow and arrow through her head.

Lindsay shrugged. "So, my mom said Uncle Bernie has a mean streak in him. Maybe he was mean to Jessica."

My mother stuck her head out the back door. "Girls, I'm going to run over and get Aunt Sharon's rental house ready for the movers. Want to come?"

I hopped off the railing. "Sure. Hey, Mom, I have a great idea. Something to cheer Jessica up before the party."

"What can be better than a party with Scott Randel?" Lindsay asked. "Except maybe a *life* with Scott Randel."

"Why don't Lindsay and I fix up Jessica's new bedroom? Maybe hang some pictures, buy some fresh flowers and stuff like that."

My mom smiled at the idea. "It would be nice if we unpacked a few of her things. To make it feel like home."

"We could paint Jessica's room yellow," Lindsay suggested. "Just like her room in Pittsburgh, remember? That real bright yellow?"

"Egg-yolk yellow," I laughed. Lindsay and I had spent five days up in Pittsburgh last summer. Jessica's room was big enough for all three of us to sleep there.

"Great idea. Let me call her landlord to see if he minds us painting."

"Who would mind free labor?" I laughed.

My mom was back in a few minutes, all excited with the news that we could do whatever we wanted, as long as it improved the property. As we headed down the porch stairs, I linked arms with my mother and Lindsay.

"This will be fun," I announced. "And it will make Jessica happy. By the time Jessica walks into her new room, she will be talking non-stop again."

"Right," agreed Lindsay. "And the first words

out of her mouth will be, 'Oh, thank you, Lindsay, darling cousin, for making my room so beautiful. How very thoughtful, how very considerate, how very, very Lindsay of you. I am so — ' "

I covered her mouth. "Jessica will spin around the room, saying, 'Oh, Callie, I know you had to be responsible for this. You should be a decorator, you have such mar-ve-lous taste.' "

By the time Lindsay and I had climbed into the back seat of Mom's car, we had decided to go straight to the paint store and buy egg-yolk yellow, the brighter the better.

"Girls, don't get your hopes up," Mom warned as she headed down the driveway. "Jessica's doctor said she may not feel like talking for a few weeks."

"A few weeks?" Lindsay rolled her eyes.

"It won't last that long, Mom," I said, my voice filled with confidence. "The moment Jessica sees her new room, she'll start talking again."

"You mean, the moment she sees us," laughed Lindsay. "Jessica won't need that psychologist anymore."

"Dr. Callie is signing up for the case. Things will be okay once they get here, trust me. My medicine is foolproof."

"Doctor Di-vine!" hooted Lindsay. "No case is too tough. No patient too sick."

We gave each other a high five. When I settled

back against the seat, I flashed my mom a big smile in the rearview mirror. I wanted her to trust me, too.

Mom was too busy chewing her lip to smile back. I kept my confident smile plastered on my face all the way to the hardware store. I didn't understand how someone could just stop talking to her friends and family, especially her own mother. But I wasn't going to let it worry me too much. After all, underneath all that silence, it was still just Jessica.

3

The next afternoon, Aunt Sharon called from Ohio. She and Jessica were finally on their way, due to arrive in Sweetwater before dark on Thursday.

We worked even faster on Jessica's room. A few uncles replastered some nicks in the wall, and two aunts volunteered to help paint. By Wednesday afternoon, we had all four walls painted.

"This is going to work out great, Callie!" said Lindsay. "We can show Jessica her room, get her talking, and still arrange for our party to start at seven-thirty, Saturday night."

I nodded, looking around the room. For a small bedroom, it sure was taking a long time to paint. The trim work still wasn't finished. I put my paintbrush down and squinted my eyes. Even with my eyes half closed, Jessica's new bedroom didn't look a bit like her fancy room in Pittsburgh.

"Lindsay, do you think we'll be able to finish the trim today?"

"We'll be finished," said Lindsay, dipping her brush back into the can of egg-yolk yellow. "My dad said to save any leftover trim for him. He doesn't want his sweet little daughter to get too tired." Lindsay made a slight bow. "I am so very del-i-cate, you know."

"Yeah, I noticed how *delicately* you wolfed down four pieces of pizza this afternoon." I picked up my brush. "I guess I just didn't realize how many walls a bedroom has."

Lindsay laughed. "Most bedrooms have four walls, Callie. At least they're finished. Trim work is so slow."

"Guess so." My back was killing me and my shoulder blades felt like they were on fire. I didn't mind doing the work; I was glad to be able to do something to make Jessica feel better. But it sure was taking a long time on such a hot day.

"We're almost finished. We can't stop now," reminded Lindsay. "Remember, this room has to be an exact duplicate of the one Jessica left in Pittsburgh."

"I know."

The moving men had arrived early that morning and were almost finished setting up the downstairs. It was starting to look less like a rental house, and more like a home. Any minute now they would be lugging bedroom furniture up the narrow staircase.

"We've almost finished the walls," Lindsay said

brightly. "And we didn't run out of paint."

"I'm glad my mom found Jessica's bedspread." My mother had been downstairs for hours, unpacking boxes and setting things in place.

Lindsay shrugged. "I just hope the moving men can get Jessica's bed up the staircase."

Jessica's bed! "Oh, my gosh, Lindsay. Jessica's bed is huge! It's a wooden tank! It will never fit into this tiny room."

Lindsay looked worried. She lowered her paintbrush and slowly turned around. "That's right. Her bed is that . . . that big wooden tank her dad made, with bookshelves and storage compartments, and that bench at the end."

I sat down heavily on top of a paint can. "This room is not going to work. We should have painted the bigger room for Jessica."

"But Aunt Sharon has all that big furniture from Great-Aunt Judy." Lindsay started painting faster. "Hurry up, Callie. Let's get the walls done and then maybe ask the moving men to leave part of Jessica's bed in the van."

I giggled. "Sure, like the mattress?"

"No, but maybe all that headboard stuff. Jessica doesn't need bookshelves. And they can store the bench in the garage for ten or twenty years."

"Jessica won't be happy about this," I said, remembering how proud she had been when her dad built it all by himself.

"Jessica loves to read, but she can leave her

books down in the living room. There are lots of shelves down there."

"Right. And we can tell the movers to put Jessica's doll house in the dining room, by the big window," I added. "As long as she has a bed and a dresser in here. The basics."

"Sure." Lindsay turned to me. "There may not be room for her desk and chair, either. The main thing is, the room looks a lot cheerier, don't you think?"

I glanced around at the bright room. Once the curtains were up and the bed was in, it would definitely look more like a bedroom.

"Thanks for helping, Lindsay. I couldn't have done all this without you."

Lindsay grinned. "I'm pretty wonderful. But hey, what are cousins for?"

We both got back to work, and by the time my mother flicked on the overhead light, we were almost finished.

"It looks great," she said. "You girls work fast!"

"Hey, you girls ready? We're ready to get started in here," came a deep voice from the hall.

"The windowsills are still wet," cried Lindsay.

"So, we'll be careful," shouted the man as he carried in Jessica's dresser. "Just get those paint cans out of the way."

"Mom, does it look okay?" I bent down and started rolling up the dropcloths. "Will Jessica like it?"

"Of course." Mom looked around the room. "The curtains and rugs will brighten it up," promised Mom. She picked up the paint cans and pounded the lids back on. "Rinse out your brushes in the basement. We'd better get out of the movers' way."

Lindsay and I sat on the small front porch, swatting mosquitoes and watching the movers drag Jessica's huge bed from the van. It took them a long time to carry the heavy pieces up the stairs, and even longer to carry the pieces that wouldn't fit back downstairs.

"What do you want us to do with all this extra stuff?" asked the driver.

"Put it in the garage," Mom suggested. "They may get a larger house later on."

Lindsay and I turned on the porch lights and watched as the rest of the furniture went up the stairs.

"With all the furniture in the garage, there's no room for Aunt Sharon's car, Mom," I pointed out.

Mom shook her head, brushing back her damp hair. "It will all work out, Callie."

"I'd better run," said Lindsay. "I promised I would be home before dark. Talk to you tomorrow, Callie."

I watched as Lindsay picked up her bike near the hedge and pedaled off toward home.

"Are you sure it will all work out fine, Mom?" I asked.

Mom reached out and patted my leg. "Yes. We can come back and fix up the house some more tomorrow."

I glanced back at the small house, at Jessica's bright yellow room glaring out from the two small windows upstairs.

I wanted it to work out. I was so excited about Jessica moving down, I could hardly wait to see my cousin again. I wanted her to like her house, to like Sweetwater, and most of all, to love living right down the block from her cousins.

4

Late Thursday, Lindsay and I packed a picnic supper and ate on Aunt Sharon's front porch. We didn't want to risk missing Jessica pull into the driveway of her new home.

"Does the welcome banner look nice?" I asked Lindsay for the fifth time.

Lindsay bit into her chicken sandwich and nodded.

I set down my sandwich. I was too nervous to eat. Then I walked down the sidewalk and turned to look at the house, pretending I was Jessica, seeing it for the first time. The house was much smaller than their house in Pittsburgh, but with the freshly planted geraniums and the four-foot welcome sign, it looked great.

"Oh, my gosh, here they come!" Lindsay stood up so fast, her apple rolled off her lap and across the porch.

I spun around, waving at the gray Volvo. Aunt Sharon's hand shot out the window from the driver's side, but Jessica sat as still as stone in the passenger seat.

"It's about time!" shouted Lindsay. She leapt up and raced toward the driveway. "I thought I was going to have to start sixth grade all by myself."

"Welcome to Sweetwater!" I called out. I walked slowly to the car, wearing a big smile, but mostly trying to look through the windshield at Jessica. Why wasn't she getting out of the car?

"Oh, come give me a hug!" cried Aunt Sharon. She hurried out of the car and swept both of us into her arms.

"Hi, Aunt Sharon," I said. I pulled away and stuck my head into the driver's side of the car. "Hi, Jessica. I bet you need to get out and stretch your legs."

Jessica looked at me for a second, then glanced down at the floor as she opened the car door and got out. She looked taller, and lots thinner than she had at Christmas.

"Hey, Jessica, get over here and give me a hug!" ordered Lindsay.

Jessica seemed to shrink up against the side of the car as Lindsay ran over and hugged her.

"How was the trip, Jessica?" she asked.

Jessica barely shrugged. I watched her face, hoping she would look at me. We'd always joked about how bold Lindsay was.

"Jessica is exhausted," Aunt Sharon said

quickly. "The trip was a lot longer than I had remembered."

"Well, you're here now," I said cheerfully.

Aunt Sharon opened the back door and pulled out a small suitcase. "Did the movers get here all right?"

"Yes. Yesterday," I said. "Everyone came over to help set things up. Mom said to call her as soon as you get a minute."

Aunt Sharon walked around and took Jessica's hand. "It was so nice of your mom to find us this house, Callie. It really helped a lot. Come on, Jessica. Let's go see our new home, honey."

Jessica followed her mother up to the front door. She glanced briefly at the porch and then walked inside.

"It looks great!" Aunt Sharon's voice was cheerful. Maybe too cheerful. She had to notice right away that she had way too much furniture for such a small house.

"Some of the stuff is in the garage," Lindsay pointed out. "Like your big oak kitchen table. It wouldn't fit in your tiny kitchen. My dad loaned you one of our card tables and he said . . ."

Aunt Sharon's face fell a second before she started smiling again. "Oh, that's fine."

"Want to see your room, Jessica?" I asked. Jessica was leaning against the doorway, looking around the crowded rooms.

"Of course she does," cried Aunt Sharon. "You

three go on up and let me freshen up a little bit."
Aunt Sharon opened a hall closet. "Do you girls
know where the powder room is?"

"The bathroom is upstairs," I said.

Aunt Sharon walked by, giving Jessica a slight
push. "Go on up, honey. You'll finally be able to
relax in your own room."

"Come on, Jessica," said Lindsay. "Wait till you
see the surprise Callie and I have for you."

Jessica looked over at me, an interested look
darting across her face for a brief second.

"Yeah, and I bet you're remembering your
Christmas surprise, right, Jessica?" I started to
laugh, hoping Jessica would smile again. "Remember last Christmas when we filled your stock-
ing with that huge rubber rattlesnake?"

"You screamed so loud!" laughed Lindsay. "And
remember when my little brothers tried to make
you a fruitcake and added whole bananas and tan-
gerines? Sick!"

"It did look good," I added fairly, starting to
giggle.

Jessica just nodded, as if nothing had been
funny about the fruitcake, and started up the
stairs.

Lindsay followed Jessica, turning to roll her
eyes at me as she jerked her thumb toward Jessica. Jessica was acting so weird.

"Your room is the first one on the left, Jessica,"
I called out.

"But wait for us," Lindsay cried. She scooted in front of Jessica and pulled the bedroom door closed. "This has to be done the right way."

"Of course." I agreed cheerfully.

Lindsay and I stood in front of the closed door, while Jessica stood silently in the hall.

"Now, Callie and I, as your favorite cousins," began Lindsay in a loud voice, "have redecorated your bedroom so that it looks just like your room in Pittsburgh."

Jessica's eyes brightened. She took a step forward and smiled. My heart started to beat faster. It was going to work, after all. All those hours of painting and cleaning had been worth it.

"So, close your eyes and get ready for your big surprise!" Lindsay waited till Jessica closed her eyes and then twisted the doorknob and let the door fly open. "Ta-daaaaaa!"

I stepped inside, still watching Jessica. Her eyes widened and her mouth fell open. She looked around the bright, egg-yolk yellow room and stared at the curtains blowing gently in the breeze, at the freshly starched bedspread piled high with as many stuffed animals as we could unpack.

"Isn't it great?" asked Lindsay. She flicked on the overhead light and then stood back, her arms outstretched like the ringmaster at the circus.

"What do you think, Jessica?" I stepped back so she could walk around. "It's a little smaller than your bedroom in Pittsburgh, but it's real cozy and . . ."

Jessica's eyes continued to dart around the room. Her mouth was still open, but she wasn't saying a word.

"She loves it," Aunt Sharon said from the doorway. She stepped inside and wrapped her arms around Jessica's shoulders. "Thanks so much, girls. How thoughtful."

"We hope you like it, Jessica," I said finally.

Jessica finally closed her mouth. She walked to the edge of her bed and sat down. After a second, she leaned back and closed her eyes.

"Jessica is exhausted," said Aunt Sharon.

"I'll bet. Come on, Lindsay, we've got to get going," I said quickly. I reached out and grabbed her by the arm. "We're late."

"For what?" Lindsay asked. "Where are we going?"

I had already dragged her down the stairs and outside before I answered her. "Hurry up."

"Why? Where are we going?" Lindsay pulled her arm from me and frowned.

"We've got to go back to my house and think up another plan," I said. "Jessica is worse than I thought."

"She *was* acting a little weird," muttered Lindsay. "She didn't even mention the welcome banner."

"Unless we think of something fast, Jessica isn't going to stick around long enough to feel welcomed."

"What? What are you talking about?"

I stopped walking and put my hands on my hips. "Lindsay, didn't you take a good look at her? Jessica is acting like some sort of zombie and Aunt Sharon looks like she's lost twenty pounds. Unless we find a way to unpack the old Jessica, there's no way they'll stay in Sweetwater past the summer."

Lindsay finally began to look worried. "Where will they go?"

"I don't know. Back to Pittsburgh, I guess. Maybe Aunt Sharon will want Jessica to go to a school to learn sign language."

"Sign language?" squeaked Lindsay. "That's for deaf people, for people who can't talk."

I sighed. "Exactly. In case you haven't noticed, our cousin Jessica doesn't talk anymore."

Lindsay grabbed my arm. "But you said she would start again, Callie."

"I know I did, Lindsay. But that was yesterday."

"So?"

I sighed again. "She's not a bit like the old Jessica."

We walked in silence as we cut through backyards, ending up in my own.

"Maybe your mom will figure out something to help Jessica," offered Lindsay.

"Maybe," I said. But my voice was barely above a whisper, not loud enough for either one of us to believe it.

5

As soon as I told my parents Aunt Sharon was at the new house, they grabbed a fresh apple pie and a frozen pizza and hopped in the car. That left Lindsay and me alone to figure out what to do about Jessica. I popped an enormous bowl of popcorn and set it down in front of Lindsay.

"We've got to come up with some plans, Lindsay. First of all, we *definitely* have to have the party on Saturday."

"In two days?" Lindsay reached for a huge handful of popcorn. "Your mom said Jessica needs more time."

"You saw Jessica tonight," I said. "We can't *wait* a week or two. It will be too late. If we give her any more time, she'll turn into a statue."

Lindsay sighed. "I guess you're right, Callie, but . . ."

"But, what?"

Lindsay leaned across the table and lowered her voice.

"Well, it's going to be a little embarrassing to have Jessica walking around our friends acting like a zombie."

"Nobody can stay quiet at a good party, Lindsay. Not even Jessica."

"But what if she does?" insisted Lindsay. "What are we going to say to our friends? 'Excuse our cousin, she left her voice in Pittsburgh'?"

"We'll have to stick by her, answer questions for her, like Aunt Sharon does. No one will even notice her not talking," I said. "They'll think Jessica is just being shy."

Lindsay giggled. "What if Scott asks her to dance and she just stands there?"

"Then *you* rush over and dance with him."

Lindsay smiled. "Gosh, what a sacrifice! All right. But what if MaryBeth or Becky asks Jessica how she likes Sweetwater?"

"We'll say, 'Oh, she loves it.' Then stick a bowl of chips in their hands."

Lindsay shook her head. "Wow, this party is going to be a lot of work."

I tapped my pencil against the tablet. "Okay, so I'll convince my mom that Jessica really wants this party, and then we can shop for food on Saturday afternoon. Do you think we should bring Jessica with us?"

Lindsay nodded. "Sure, maybe we can get her to start talking before the party starts."

"Yeah!" Suddenly I had a great idea. "Let's go

through our photo albums and get as many pictures of Jessica with her cousins as we can. We can make her a scrapbook. That will remind her of all the great memories we've had together down here."

Lindsay leaned across the table and grabbed my hand. "You are one smart kid, Callie."

I grinned. "But, of course. And after we shop on Saturday, let's stop by your house so Jessica can visit the twins."

"Oh, yeah." Lindsay laughed. "Nothing like spending a few hectic, quality hours at *my* house with a pair of five-year-old wild boys. Jessica might just crawl into a coma."

"Your brothers are cute," I insisted. "And Jessica thinks they are adorable. Remember how she made them those animal puppets for Christmas? She always talks to them."

"She *used* to talk to them." Lindsay frowned. "But, she used to talk to us, too."

I got up, thunderstruck with another great idea. "How about if the twins put on a puppet show? Yeah, and their puppets will talk about how much they love having Jessica back. And, then, the puppets will ask Jessica to say hello."

Lindsay frowned. "But, Jessica *won't* say hello. Then the twins will start screaming for her to answer their dumb puppets and finally they will crawl out from behind the counter and throw their puppets on the floor."

I smiled. "No they won't. Your little brothers love Jessica."

"Oh, okay, so they aren't complete monsters. I just don't know if it's going to work."

"Lindsay, what do we have to lose?"

Lindsay shrugged.

The answer hit me hard. I knew what we had to lose if we didn't keep trying.

Jessica.

6

Friday was a very long day. I spent most of the afternoon cleaning the game room, organizing my tapes, and setting up the volleyball net. I didn't call or walk over to see Jessica. I didn't have enough energy for it. I figured she needed time to unpack and relax.

On Saturday morning, I walked over and got Lindsay to go shopping for the party. Mom had given me some money and I added ten bucks of my own baby-sitting cash. In order to get to Lindsay's, I had to walk past Jessica's house. I crossed the street and ran past, too chicken to be with Jessica alone. When someone isn't adding a single word to the conversation, your own voice starts to sound a little loud.

I was glad Lindsay wasn't a bit nervous. In fact, she was *calm.*

"Relax, Callie," Lindsay said. She was all dressed up with new shorts and twenty-nine silver bracelets clattering on her arms. "You never know who you'll see at the Winn Dixie," she laughed.

As Lindsay and I walked back to get Jessica, we discussed our agenda like two generals marching into battle.

"So, after the food shopping, we go back to your house," I said. "Are your brothers ready to do the puppet show?"

Lindsay gave a gloomy nod. "Yeah, but I had to pay them each a dollar."

"Are you sure they know what to say?"

"They should. I wrote out a little script and rehearsed it with them two times. I told them if they blew it, I'd take back the money."

We talked about the party, too. Lindsay was going to stay with Jessica for the first hour of the party, and then I was going to take my shift. With any luck, Jessica would be talking by ten o'clock and we could all relax and enjoy the party.

Aunt Sharon was pleased when we knocked on the door and asked Jessica to walk into town with us.

"Jessica would absolutely love to walk into town with you," cried Aunt Sharon. "She'd be thrilled to get out of this house."

Jessica didn't look too thrilled. She looked kind of scared when we told her about the party. Of course, since she wasn't talking to us, she couldn't tell us she wasn't coming. Aunt Sharon popped in and said Jessica would be *thrilled* to come.

"Scott Randel said to say hello to you," Lindsay said cheerfully as we headed into town. "He is cuter than ever. He's about five-six now and he wears glasses that make him look like a handsome doctor."

Jessica shot us both a look at the word *doctor*, like she was wondering if we knew that she had gone to see a psychologist. I wanted to tell her that I went to see a psychologist once, right after my gramma died. But it's hard to bring personal stuff up with someone who isn't even talking to you. So I didn't.

Lindsay held up her arm and jingled the bracelets. "If you want to borrow any of my clothes or stuff, just ask, Jessica."

Jessica shoved up the sleeves of her cotton shirt and shook her head.

"Jessica has more clothes than both of us put together," I said quickly. I elbowed Lindsay.

"Hey, what did I do?" Lindsay sounded mad. "I wasn't implying Jessica looked like a slob, I was just trying to be nice."

I laughed louder. "Oh, we know that. Don't we, Jessica?"

Luckily, the store was in sight, so the three of us walked inside silently. With all the noise surrounding us, I was able to relax a little.

Lindsay pushed the big metal cart and Jessica and I followed. "All the kids coming tonight are real nice, Jessica," I promised. "It will be fun. And Lindsay and I will be right beside you. In case you get nervous."

"Oh, Jessica loves parties," laughed Lindsay. "Remember that Fourth of July party last summer, Jessie? When you put those plastic ice cubes with the spiders into the punch bowl? That was so funny."

Jessica smiled a little.

"We have to get lots of food," I said. "Do you have any favorite snacks, Jessica?"

Jessica shrugged.

"Chips and pretzels sound good," I answered. "And my mom said she'd order four large pizzas. What should we get on them?" I deliberately looked at Jessica, knowing she loved green peppers and mushrooms.

Jessica just shrugged again, looking off across the produce section.

"Pepperoni on two, and just cheese on the other two," Lindsay finally decided. She winked at me, telling me she remembered about the green peppers and mushrooms, too.

"That sound okay to you, Jessica?" she asked loudly.

Jessica nodded, shoving her hands deep into her pockets. I felt a little sorry for her then, wondering what she was so busy thinking about that she didn't want to talk.

"Maybe one with green peppers and mushrooms," I said at last.

"And we have to borrow some more outdoor candles," reminded Lindsay. "My brothers chewed the wicks off half of ours."

Jessica looked up at the mention of the twins. Lindsay's little brothers were identical, with bright red hair and cinnamon freckles.

"Let's stop by on the way home and leave the food at your house," I said casually. "Your mom can drive it over later."

Lindsay smiled. "Why, that's a great idea, Callie." We had rehearsed how we were going to get Jessica over to Lindsay's house at least five times already.

"Yes, sir. That sounds like a *real* good idea," assured Lindsay. "My brothers were asking when you'd be able to stop by, Jessica. They have a surprise for you."

For the next hour we pushed the cart around the Winn Dixie, tossing in potato chips, bags of thick pretzels, lemonade mix, and three large tubs of dip. While Lindsay and I ran down aisle three to get some napkins and paper plates, Jessica stayed by the cart.

"What if she runs away?" hissed Lindsay as we hurried back up the aisle. "She won't be able to ask for directions."

"She won't," I said. "Where would she go?"

When we got back, Jessica was just finishing with the cart. She had completely organized everything into neat sections. There was plenty of room left for the plates and napkins.

"Gosh, Jessica," laughed Lindsay. "I had forgotten what a neat *freak* you were."

The word *freak* came out too loudly. I elbowed Lindsay.

"I'll bet you keep your locker at school real neat, too," I said quickly, wanting to get past the freak business.

Jessica shoved her hands back into her pockets and started walking toward the checkout. I motioned for Lindsay to walk on ahead with her, spinning my fingers in front of my mouth to remind her to talk to Jessica.

"So, Jessica, did I tell you who all was coming tonight?" Lindsay said. She walked up and slung her arm around Jessica's shoulders. Jessica's back straightened, but she didn't fling off Lindsay's arm.

The grocery bags were heavy on the long walk back to Lindsay's house.

"Why didn't we think to bring the wagon?" groaned Lindsay.

"Only four more blocks." I nudged Jessica with my elbow. "Is that bag too heavy, Jessie?"

Jessica shook her head, letting her thick dark hair fall forward, half covering her face. Jessica had been wearing her hair like that ever since she had arrived. Usually Jessica had worn her hair in elaborate French braids, or a high, short pony-tail.

We were all silent for the rest of the walk home.

"At last," Lindsay panted. She stumbled up her front steps and sank into a cushioned chair. "Get me some ice-cold lemonade, Callie. Jessica, get me a cold rag for my head."

I started to smile. "Sure, Lindsay. In your dreams."

I picked up Lindsay's bag of groceries and walked into the cool kitchen. I could smell brownies.

"Aunt Shelly is making her famous brownies for your welcome home party, Jessica," I said. "Isn't that nice?"

Jessica let her grocery bag thump onto the kitchen table. She slid into a chair and pushed back her hair.

"It sure is hot in Sweetwater, isn't it?" I sat down in the chair across from her. "You should wear your hair up in a French braid tonight, Jessica. It would be cooler."

At first I thought Jessica was going to say something back to me. Her mouth opened and she leaned forward. But then she got a real sad look on her face and stood up.

"Hey, look, Conner, it's Jessica!"

Lindsay's twin brothers raced into the room, hurling their wirey arms around Jessica's waist. They started to hop up and down and, in between their shouts, I could have sworn I heard Jessica laughing.

7

"**I** didn't hear her laugh," said Lindsay. "It was just the twins being the twins."

I grabbed the tray filled with lemonade and pretzels and headed into the living room. I know what I saw and heard, and Jessica was definitely glad to be around Connor and Casey. She didn't say anything, but I could tell she was impressed to see the puppet theater the boys had created out of boxes and an old shower curtain.

"Okay, now Callie, you and Lindsay sit down next to Jessica," instructed Connor. "Casey will come by and collect tickets in just a minute."

"What tickets?" I asked.

"First, you got to go get a ticket from Casey so he can collect it," explained Connor. "He's selling them in the bathroom. For free."

Lindsay groaned. "Come on, boys. Let's get this show on the road."

But Jessica was already heading down the hall to the bathroom-ticket-counter, so I got up and followed.

"Do you want a seat on the couch, or a seat on a kitchen chair, Jessica?" asked Casey.

Jessica shrugged. Casey was sitting on a stool in the middle of the tub, wearing a baseball cap backwards and a pair of sunglasses with the lenses popped out.

"Which one?" repeated Casey.

Jessica glanced back at me, her cheeks reddening. I wondered if this would be when she would start to speak.

"How about a couch seat," suggested Casey, holding out a slip of paper. "Next!"

"I'd like a couch seat, too," I said. "An aisle seat, please."

"We don't got no aisle seats, Callie," said Casey. "Just a chair or a couch."

"Couch will be fine, thanks."

Lindsay reached out her hand. "I'll take the chair, Casey."

Casey drew the shower curtain closed. "Sorry, lady. This show is all sold out."

"What?" Lindsay drew back the shower curtain. "Give me a ticket, Casey."

Casey drew back the curtain and giggled. "Sorry. The next show starts at dinnertime."

"Unreal," muttered Lindsay, storming out of the bathroom.

Jessica hopped out of the way as Casey bolted from the tub and raced down the hall. "Get your tickets ready!"

Once Jessica and I were seated on the couch, next to a large stuffed bear sitting on a kitchen chair, Casey came over and took our tickets.

"Enjoy the show," he said with a grin.

"Hey, Lindsay, you can come and watch the show, too," called Connor from behind the stage. "But you have to stand in the back and you're not allowed to smoke."

Lindsay clattered some pans in the kitchen, but as soon as the curtain was pulled, she walked in and stood by the bookshelves.

"Hello, there!" said a duck puppet. It hopped along the card table and was joined by a larger dog puppet. I was hoping Jessica would be pleased to see the twins using the puppets she had made for them.

"Hello, duck!"

"Hello, furry guy."

"Want to hear a joke?"

"Sure!"

"Go ahead."

"Go ahead and what?"

"Tell me the joke."

"What joke?"

Casey popped up from behind the table, a frown on his face. "How come you guys aren't laughing?"

43

I giggled. "Sorry, I thought the joke wasn't over yet."

Casey nodded. "I think it was."

Lindsay laughed. "That was good, boys."

Casey bent down behind the table. "Okay, furry puppet. We have a new neighbor."

"We do? Whooooooooooo?" shouted the dog puppet. "Is she a dog like me, or is she a flea?"

I laughed extra loud since Jessica hadn't moved a muscle. She was staring at the puppets as if she had never seen them before.

"Jessica is a person, not a dog. She's the new neighbor," said the duck puppet. "Hi, Jessica."

"Hi, Jessica!" cried the furry puppet. "I'm fur man. How are you?"

Jessica shifted a few times on the couch. She glanced over at me, looking kind of nervous. I guess she thought everyone knew she wasn't talking.

"Do you like our show, Jessica?" asked the dog.

"I do," I sang out. "You're nice puppets."

"Thank you, Callie."

"And I like the show, too," called out Lindsay. "Even though you gave me the cheapest seat in the house."

The twins giggled from behind the table. "And what about you, new neighbor, Jessica? Do you like our show?"

Jessica nodded.

"Do you?" asked the dog.

Jessica nodded again.

"She does," I said after another long minute. I let out a disappointed sigh. The puppet trick wasn't going to work at all. I guess cures like that only worked in the movies.

"Hey, Jessica!" Casey was standing up now, his puppet lying on the table. "Why don't you answer my puppet?"

"Yeah," Connor said, stretching his dog puppet out toward Jessica. "Hi, my name is Fido. What's your name?"

Casey pulled on his puppet again. "Do you like our show, Jessica?" Casey shook his duck puppet up and down. "Do you like it, or do you hate it?"

After a second, Casey tossed the duck puppet across the floor.

I glanced back at Lindsay. She had been right.

"I like it."

I smiled at Lindsay. At least she was trying for the twins' sake.

But Lindsay was staring at me, mouth open.

That's when I noticed it was Jessica talking, a tiny yellow duck puppet on her hand.

8

"Three words, Callie," pointed out Lindsay. "That's all Jessica said. Then she clammed up again, back to her old zombie self."

I moved the nail polish closer to me and smiled. Lindsay refused to be as overjoyed as I was about Jessica actually talking! Three words was a lot for someone who hadn't said a word in three weeks.

"If you spill that polish on my rug, my mom will kill you," said Lindsay. She stretched her arms over her head and yawned. "Boy, Jessica couldn't wait to get out of here after that puppet show."

"Maybe she wants to spend a long time getting ready for our wonderful party."

"Yeah, right, Callie. Don't be surprised if the phone rings and Aunt Sharon tells us that Jessica has locked herself in the hall closet and she won't come out."

"Lindsay," I cried, swatting her with my dry hand. "Why are you being this way? I thought you would be happy to know that your puppet show worked."

"Because it *didn't* work, Callie," said Lindsay. "She said three words, actually, the *duck* said three words, and then she got up and walked home." Lindsay leaned against her bed and rolled her eyes. "I don't call that a permanent cure, Dr. Di-vine."

I could feel my temper warming up. Jessica had talked and it *was* a big deal! "So, what would you call it, then, Miss Know-it-all-Lindsay?"

Lindsay shrugged. "A duck talked."

"But, Jessica *is* the duck," I sputtered.

Lindsay started to laugh. "Gosh. And here I was thinking it was really the duck."

"You're putting me in a bad mood," I warned, dabbing a spot of Bubble-Gum Pink on each nail. "I think we have made a real breakthrough on the Jessica case, and you're acting like a big jerk about it."

"A big jerk?" asked Lindsay, raising one eyebrow. "Is that a medical term, doctor?"

"Yes," I snapped back. "Jerk, it's Latin for . . . for a girl who wants our party to be a flop."

Lindsay looked surprised. "Callie, I think you're a . . ."

"A what?" I knew I was acting like an even bigger jerk, but Lindsay was really getting on my nerves with her negative thoughts. Why couldn't she be happy about Jessica, too?

47

"You're a dreamer," said Lindsay. She wasn't smiling now. "You want to believe Jessica is going to be okay, but maybe she isn't."

"She is, too."

Lindsay got up and closed her bedroom door. "My mom said that Aunt Sharon is making another appointment for Jessica with a doctor in Pittsburgh. They're going to fly up next week and try to get Uncle Bernie to come, too."

"What?" Wasn't Uncle Bernie the reason Jessica had stopped talking in the first place? Why would Aunt Sharon want him hanging around again?

Lindsay stretched out on her bed and picked up her Mickey Mouse alarm clock. "The party starts in two hours, Callie."

"I know. I'm going to leave as soon as my nails dry."

"Callie, are you nervous about tonight?"

I laughed. "Nervous? Lindsay, this party is no big deal. We see these kids every day during school."

"I know. But, what if our friends think Jessica is weird?"

I shrugged. "They won't."

"But, they might, Callie. She's our cousin, and I really like her, but I don't like being around her the way she is right now." Lindsay got up and started to pace around the room. "Don't get mad at me, Callie, 'cause I'm just being honest. But,

48

Jessica isn't fun to be around. She makes me nervous."

"Oh, well I'll talk to her about it, Lindsay." I stood up and thumped the nail polish down on her dresser. "I'll tell her to shape up so you will enjoy her company."

"I asked you not to get mad," wailed Lindsay. "I was just being honest."

"Well, be honest with someone else, then, Lindsay," I snapped. "Because cousins don't give up on cousins, okay?"

"You're mad at me now," pointed out Lindsay. "So, doesn't that mean you're giving up on me?"

I was stunned for a second, wondering if Lindsay was right. I glanced at her alarm clock, frowning at how happy Mickey looked. What a stupid mouse. He didn't have a clue how complicated life could be.

"No, I'm not," I muttered. "See you tonight."

"See you," said Lindsay.

But, she didn't walk me downstairs and she didn't give me one of her goofy grins. So maybe she was getting ready to give up on me, too.

9

Lindsay was twenty minutes late for our party. I started getting nervous. Maybe she *was* mad at me. What if Lindsay wasn't going to show up? That would leave me the only one in charge of Jessica.

But at ten of eight, Jessica and Lindsay came up the walk together. Lindsay was already laughing and talking with a few other kids who were just arriving. Jessica had the same look I wore when I was on my way for my allergy shots.

"It's about time," I muttered as Lindsay walked in. "Hi, Jessica, hi, Katie, Brad. Go on downstairs. Cold drinks are in the cooler."

I kept my hand on Lindsay's arm. I wanted to tell her that we should call a truce on fighting with each other. No matter what might happen with Jessica, Lindsay was my most favorite friend and cousin in the world. I turned to grab onto Jessica, so we could all walk downstairs together, but she

50

must have been swept away with another arrival of kids.

"She'll be okay for a few minutes," said Lindsay. She patted her pocket. "I have a surprise for you, Callie."

"I have one for you, too," I said quickly. "An apology."

Lindsay made a big deal about acting shocked and sliding down the refrigerator like it was the first time I had ever apologized to anyone in my life. I mean, I'm not *that* bad. When you have a temper like mine, you end up apologizing more often than most people.

"I'm sorry I got mad at you for being honest with me," I said. I grinned. "And you're not a jerk. I mean, not all the time."

Lindsay smiled back. "Thanks. And you are a dreamer but . . ." Lindsay patted her pocket again. "I thought I'd bring a little bit of your dream to the party in case we need it."

"What?" I reached into Lindsay's pocket and pulled out the duck puppet. "Who invited him?"

"Jessica only talks when the duck is around," Lindsay said simply. "So, maybe she might like seeing a friendly face."

I started to laugh. "I don't know about this one, Lindsay."

Lindsay snatched back the duck and put it in her pocket. "You're not the only one with good ideas, Callie. By the end of the party, you will be down on your knees, thanking me for bringing Mr. Duck."

"Mr. Duck?"

More kids came in the side door. Lindsay and I headed downstairs with them. I was glad to hear the music and laughing downstairs. At least it sounded like a regular party so far.

"How have you been, Callie?" asked MaryBeth. She was starting seventh grade with me in the fall. "I just got back from camp last night."

"I'm fine," I shouted over the music. "Did you meet my cousin, Jessica? She just moved here."

MaryBeth walked over with me to the chair Jessica had sunk into.

"Jessica, this is MaryBeth Johnson. She lives five houses down from you."

"Hi, Jessica," said MaryBeth. She sat down on the edge of the chair. "Did you meet the family with ten kids that lives behind you, yet?"

Jessica shook her head.

"Well, if they ask you to baby-sit, say no," laughed MaryBeth. "They're crazy."

Jessica turned her head away from MaryBeth. But, MaryBeth was up and off the chair, chasing after one of her younger sister's friends.

"MaryBeth is real popular in school," I told Jessica. I wasn't sure why I was tacking on that bit of information. Maybe to let Jessica know that it was important to be nice to these kids. They could make life easier, or more difficult, once school started.

"Dip?" Lindsay shoved the tray into my hand.

"Are you calling me names again?" I asked. Lindsay and I both howled at that one, but Jessica only sighed.

"Hey, go get the volleyball game started, Callie," said Lindsay. She tapped her watch, reminding me that she had signed up for the first shift with Jessica.

"Oh, okay. And, you two come on outside if you want to play." Jessica was watching the kids through the big picture window. "Or, you guys can just watch."

The party got real loud once the volleyball game started. Scott and his loony friends had water pistols and pretty soon a range war had broken out.

"Scott soaked me!" wailed MaryBeth. She pulled her wet hair back from her face. She didn't look the least bit mad.

Jessica and I were sitting on top of the picnic table, watching everyone else have fun. It was already nine-fifteen. My mom had just phoned in the pizza order and my dad had turned on the outside flood lights.

"Nice party," said MaryBeth.

"Thanks," I said. Actually, I was feeling a little sorry for myself. A few kids had come over to say hello, but once they realized Jessica wasn't talking to them, they made up some excuse to go to another group. Even though I was trying to stick by her, I couldn't help but be bored stiff. It was like sitting by myself. I was tired of thinking up polite, dumb stuff to say to Jessica.

"I'm going to go dry off," said MaryBeth. I watched her head for the house, but halfway there, she joined another group and they all took off, racing after other kids.

"Do you two have some contagious disease?"

I looked up and tried to smile at Scott. Actually, I was beginning to feel like I did have something wrong with me. Like maybe I was choking on all that I had bitten off with Jessica.

"Want to shoot some hoops, Jessica?" asked Scott. He looked at me and smiled, like he knew I would be proud of him for showing off his nice manners.

Jessica smiled at Scott a little. I knew she remembered him. Lindsay was always talking about Scott.

"Want to, Jessica?" I asked. "I'll come, too."

Scott laughed. "Are you the chaperone tonight, Callie?"

I made a face. Boy, if he only knew.

"Hey, Scott, we're picking teams," shouted Brad. "Get over here."

"Want to play?" Scott asked again. He gave Jessica a smile that would have melted Lindsay to the table.

Jessica glanced at me for a second. I didn't know if she wanted me to say yes for her or not. So I just shrugged. Jessica, I wanted to say, I am not a mind reader.

As soon as Scott left, Jessica's face fell. I guess she did want to play after all. I was about to drag her over there when I had a better idea.

10

I wove my way through the crowd, grabbed two cans of Coke from the cooler, and then grabbed Lindsay from behind.

"Yeow," cried Lindsay, hopping back. "Your hands are like ice, lady. Where's Jessica? It's your shift, isn't it?"

"She's over by the picnic table," I explained. "I have a plan."

"Oh, great," groaned Lindsay. "Plan number fifty-three going into action."

I smiled. "Yeah, but *this* plan is going to work. Just you watch."

"Yeah, sure. My eyes will be glued to you."

I held out my hand and grinned. "Just keep your eyes on the duck."

Lindsay took over my shift with Jessica while I tried to put the duck plan in motion. I hoped it would work. I was getting tired of baby-sitting Jessica. Being loyal to a cousin was one thing, but being her full-time bodyguard was too demanding. I hadn't been able to enjoy my own party.

"Scott, can I talk to you a minute?" I kept Mr. Duck behind my back.

"Watch this, Callie!" shouted Scott, charging the hoop and completing a smooth lay-up.

After watching a few more shots, I grabbed Scott and pulled him beside the hedge.

"Easy, Callie," laughed Scott. "I had no idea my basketball was going to have this effect on you!"

"Scott, you have no effect on me. But, I have a favor to ask." Scott was used to having girls trailing after him, and I decided to let him know right off the bat that I wasn't one of them.

Scott nodded. "Sure, Callie, what? You want a few private lessons for slam dunking?"

"No. I want you to ask Jessica to sit and eat pizza with you."

Scott shrugged. "Sure. She can sit with us. No problem."

My fingers squeezed around the puppet. "Well, actually, there *is* a problem, Scott. It's pretty serious."

Scott shot me his famous Randel smile. If I hadn't known this kid since he was two, wearing a soggy diaper, I might have been impressed.

"What problem, Callie? Is Jessica some sort of serial killer?"

I glanced over at Jessica. She was slumped on the picnic bench. "Jessica wouldn't hurt a fly. She weighs eighty pounds."

Scott hooted. "So what? You think all serial killers are overweight?"

While Scott was laughing hard over his own joke, I whipped out Mr. Duck. Scott stopped laughing and pointed to the puppet.

"Who's this?"

"Mr. Duck. He's a puppet."

Scott winked. "And I thought he was another relative of yours, Callie."

I was getting nowhere fast. I had to let Scott know I was serious. I put my hand on his arm.

"Scott, there's a real problem with Jessica. Haven't you noticed something odd about her?"

Scott glanced over at the picnic table. "She's okay. Kind of quiet. Hard to believe she's related to you and Lindsay."

"Jessica's mute."

"She's *what*?" Scott took a step back, like it might be contagious. I realized right away I shouldn't have used that term. It was too strong. Why hadn't I just said Jessica was *quiet*?

"Jessica's parents just got divorced and now she won't talk to anyone," I said quickly. "She's been to a special doctor, but he can't find a way to make her talk."

"Whoa, that's too bad," said Scott. He looked stricken. "Is she crazy or something?"

"Of course not." I swatted him with Mr. Duck. "She just needs some cheering up. Which is why I want you and Mr. Duck to help."

Scott looked at the puppet and frowned. "Mr. *Duck?*"

"Jessica will talk through the duck. She used him to talk earlier today. I don't know why it worked, but it did," I explained. "And I know she likes you." I drew in a deep breath, wondering how heavy I had to lay it on to get Scott involved. "I mean, *all* the girls like you, Scott. You know that."

Scott stood up straighter and grinned. He shifted from foot to foot. "Hey, I can't help it. What can I say?"

I held out Mr. Duck. "Just go over with Mr. Duck on your hand and ask Jessica to sit with you to eat some pizza. That's all you have to do. You can make it a game."

Scott held up both hands. "Hey, I don't play with puppets anymore, Callie. There's no way I'm going to look like a jerk in front of everyone. Ask Lindsay to do it. She likes acting silly."

"This isn't *silly*, Scott. Jessica's problem is very serious! Her doctor said if she doesn't start talking soon, she'll have to leave Sweetwater!"

"I'm not a doctor. I wouldn't know what to say to her." Scott ran his fingers through his hair. "Callie, I'll look like an idiot with this dumb duck."

I held up the tiny puppet. "Scott, no one will

even see you with Mr. Duck. It will mean so much to Jessica. She's been so sad since her dad left."

Scott paused for a second, thinking, then shook his head. "Nah. Ask someone else to do it."

I glanced around the yard. "I don't see anyone that Jessica would like to sit with."

"She can sit with you." Scott shoved his hands into his pockets. "Besides, I barely know Jessica."

Scott was right. I really couldn't blame him for not wanting to get involved. If Jessica weren't related to me, maybe I wouldn't want to, either.

"Never mind," I said finally. "It was a dumb idea, I guess. This stupid divorce has messed up so many things."

"Oh, give me the duck," Scott growled. He squeezed the puppet into a ball and hid it inside his fist. "Just don't mention this to anyone. You hear?"

"I hear," I said, smiling from ear to ear. And as I watched Scott stride across the yard to the picnic table, I laughed out loud for the first time since my party had started.

11

I caught up with Lindsay by the cooler. She was trying to fill a squirt gun with the icy water. A perfect hostess.

"Don't be mad," protested Lindsay as soon as she saw me. "I only left Jessica for a second to fill up this gun."

"I'm glad that you did leave her, Lindsay," I said. "You're a genius, cousin."

Lindsay smiled. "Good. What wonderful thing have I done now?"

I lowered my voice as I pulled Lindsay to a tall evergreen. "Scott is with Mr. Duck."

Lindsay grinned. "Is it serious?"

I giggled. "No. I told him about Jessica. How she only talks to and with puppets. So, Scott agreed to be Mr. Duck and to ask Jessica to sit with him and eat pizza."

"Wow!" Lindsay dropped her squirt gun. "That kid is too good to be true. What a nice guy!"

"Let's see what's going on," I whispered, peering out from behind the tree.

Scott was sitting on the picnic table. He must have asked Jessica something, because she was nodding and they both looked pretty embarrassed.

"*Talk*, Jessica," hissed Lindsay. "Does that girl know how many sixth-graders have a crush on Scott Randel?"

"*Shhhhhhh.*" I held my breath as Scott pulled Mr. Duck from his pocket. "He's got the puppet."

"What's he saying?" asked Lindsay, almost knocking me over as she tried to see.

"He has it on his hand. Oh, good. He's talking." I pulled down another branch. "He's laughing now. The duck is hopping up Jessica's arm, and . . ."

"Yo!" shouted Brad. "Yo, Mr. Puppet Man. What do you have there?"

I was out from behind the tree in less than a second, trying to catch up with Brad. I was too late.

Scott's face was burning red. He still wore the duck.

"Pretty impressive little show, Scott. So, where's Bert and Ernie?" hooted Brad. He grabbed Mr. Duck and tossed him up in the air. "Up you go, duckie. Hey, I have to be honest with ya, Scott. The junior high might not let you bring your toys to school."

A few more kids walked over, laughing.

"Of course," added Brad, "if your mommy writes a note, maybe you could bring them for recess time."

"Shut up, Brad. Give me the puppet," said Scott. He glared at me. Jessica glared at me, too. They were both acting as if I had personally invited Brad over to make fun of them.

"Hey, Scottie," cried Brad in a high, squeaky voice. "Do you have any food for me? Quack! Quack! How about some quackers?"

Everyone acted like that was the funniest joke they had ever heard. Even Lindsay started to laugh.

"Stop laughing, Lindsay," I snapped. I walked over and snatched the puppet from Brad. "It's my duck."

Brad grabbed it back. "Nah, this belongs to Scottie-boy. I'll bet he has a bunny rabbit and a little moo-moo cow puppet at home, too."

"Brad, you're terrible," giggled MaryBeth.

Scott stood up and brushed past Brad, his shoulder knocking Brad's. "You talk too much, Brad," Scott said angrily.

"Yeah, be quiet, Brad!" I added. "In fact, go home."

"I just got here!" Brad looked from Scott to me, then shrugged. "Hey, don't get mad at me. I was only kidding around. Gosh, you guys can't take a joke. Some party this is."

Scott relaxed a little then. He reached out and shoved Brad on the shoulder. "Sorry, man."

Brad nodded. "It's okay. Sorry if I interrupted anything."

Scott's face clouded over again. He glanced back at Jessica before shooting me a dirty look. "You didn't interrupt a thing. In fact, your timing was perfect. I just remembered I have to get home early."

"Don't go, Scott," wailed Lindsay, trailing after him. "I thought you wanted to shoot some more hoops. Come on, Scott, don't be mad."

Scott stopped being mad when so many girls begged him to stay. In fact, in a couple of minutes, the party was back to normal. The pizzas arrived and everyone started setting up tables and chairs.

"Whoa, are we lucky," whispered Lindsay. She slid a plate with two slices of cheese pizza down in front of me. "For a second there, I thought our party was going down the tubes."

"Me, too. Close call, all right."

Lindsay took a bite of pizza and nodded. "Your turn to baby-sit Jessica."

"I took a turn. Seems like I've been glued to her side all night," I cried. "I haven't even had a chance to talk to Lanie or Vanessa yet."

"Well, I wanted to play one on one with Scott." Lindsay took another bite and searched the yard. "Hey, where is she, anyway?"

I checked the picnic table, the volleyball court, and the side yard. No Jessica.

She probably went home, I thought to myself. She only lived a couple of blocks away. I went inside the house and checked all the rooms. Jessica wasn't anywhere. It was really kind of rude of her to leave without saying good-bye. Of course, these days, Jessica wasn't saying anything. I could hear the laughter outside from my other guests, the ones who were having fun at my party.

I checked the porch swing and then I gave up the search. There wasn't anything I could do about it. I had tried my best, but Jessica was gone.

Truth was, I was glad.

12

"What do you mean, she's gone?" Lindsay followed me down the porch steps.

"I mean, I've looked everywhere and Jessica isn't here anymore. She's mad about the duck." I groaned. "Oh, who knows why she's mad? She never talks, so how are we supposed to know what she's feeling? I don't know about you, Lindsay, but I am worn out."

Lindsay glanced nervously around the yard. "Maybe she's hiding somewhere," she whispered. "Listening."

"She isn't here, Lindsay. Jessica got mad and left."

"But, Callie, we were supposed to be in *charge* of her. What do you think she told Aunt Sharon?"

I grinned. "Well, since she refuses to talk, I guess she didn't tell her anything."

"I guess so."

"Yeah."

Scott came around the house. "Yo, Lindsay. Ready to finish the game?"

"I'll be right there." Lindsay nudged me. "Jessie is probably home with Aunt Sharon right now."

Scott and Lindsay went around back and I followed. I wished I could relax enough to play. I am pretty good at basketball. In fact, I am probably better at sports than with people, period. At least basketball comes with a set of rules. Kids like Jessica were a total mystery to me.

Kids started leaving at ten-thirty. Lindsay and I stood at the top of the driveway, waving good-bye and making plans to meet different kids at the park, community pool, or the mall.

"This party was so much fun, I might have to have one myself next Saturday," said MaryBeth. "Can you both come?"

"Me, too?" squeaked Lindsay. She had never been invited to MaryBeth's house before, except to drop off some Girl Scout cookies back in the third grade.

MaryBeth laughed. "Sure, you, too." MaryBeth glanced around the yard. "Listen, I don't want to be mean or anything, but . . ."

I knew what she was going to say. But I leaned forward anyway, smiling as broadly as Lindsay.

"I can't ask your cousin, Jessica, to *this* party." MaryBeth flushed a little. "It will be a small group of kids, you know, kids in our *crowd*."

Lindsay stood up straighter, as if she had just learned she was to be inducted into West Point.

MaryBeth's father flashed his headlights on and off. "Gosh, I'd better go. Don't want my dad getting mad at me when I'm about to ask to have a party." MaryBeth tossed her hair over one shoulder and waved. "See you Saturday."

"I'll be there," cried Lindsay.

" 'Bye, MaryBeth."

"I can't believe it," sighed Lindsay. "Wait till I tell my mom." Lindsay's face fell. "My mom! Oh, brother. What if my mom thinks I'm too young for a seventh-grade party?"

"Be on your best behavior all week and then tell her about the party on Thursday," I suggested.

Lindsay put her arm around my neck. "You are one smart lady, Callie."

"Thanks. You're smart to notice how smart I am. But did you know that I'm also cute, athletic, and ter-rib-ly talented at party giving?" I slung my arm around Lindsay, the two of us staggering around my driveway, laughing.

"Hi, girls! How was the party?"

"Great!" We both said at once, laughing again. It *had* been a good party.

"Good. I hope I'm not the last to pick up."

My head shot up; my smile slid off my face. It was Aunt Sharon, come to get Jessica.

13

Within fifteen minutes, four of my uncles and two of my aunts were crowded into our kitchen, quizzing Lindsay and me as if we were criminals.

"But, *when* did she leave?" asked my dad. "Come on, Callie, think!"

"I'm not sure. Before the pizza," I offered.

"Yeah," added Lindsay. "It was after Scott tried to get her to talk, and before the pizza man walked into the yard."

Aunt Sharon put her hand on my arm. "Who's Scott?"

Lindsay automatically smiled. "He is soooo nice, Aunt Sharon . . ."

"He's a kid in my class," I said quickly. "He was sitting with Jessica on the picnic table."

"What's this business about Scott trying to get Jessica to talk?" asked Uncle Lenny. "I thought she wasn't talking to anyone."

Aunt Sharon's hands were trembling as she

brushed back her hair. "She isn't. She isn't even trying."

"Did Scott upset Jessica?" my dad asked.

"No!" said Lindsay. "In fact, if Brad hadn't interrupted, I'll bet Jessica would have started talking to Mr. Duck."

I groaned, knowing I would have to tell the whole story. Sitting around the kitchen table, surrounded by my worried aunts and uncles, and a crying Aunt Sharon, I could tell it sounded pretty stupid.

"We'd better start searching the neighborhood," my mother said. She set three flashlights down on the kitchen table.

"I already called the hospitals and the police," my dad said gently. "Jessica hasn't been found."

"Oh, poor Jessica," sobbed Aunt Sharon. "Why would she run away from us? We're family."

"Maybe she's running to Uncle Bernie," I said.

"Callie! Be quiet," snapped my dad.

"I was only trying to help," I stammered.

Aunt Sharon took a napkin from the table and wiped her eyes. "Let's get going." She got up and then slid back down again in her chair. "I don't even know where to look."

"We can help," offered Lindsay. "We walked into town with Jessie today. Maybe she went there, to take a walk."

"You stay here," barked my dad. He picked up a flashlight and pointed it at me. "Both of you."

71

I hopped up from my chair. "Can't we help search the backyards? I want to help, Dad."

My dad shook his head. "You've done enough, Callie."

I sat back down and watched everyone file outside, past the party remains and up the driveway.

"We did try to help, Lindsay," I said miserably. And it wasn't my fault that Jessica ran away. So, why was I feeling so guilty?

14

Fifteen minutes later, the phone rang.

"Callie? Hi, honey, it's Mom. We found Jessie. Aunt Sharon passed her house and saw Jessica's bedroom light on. I guess she went in the back door and straight up to her room."

My knees suddenly turned to Jell-O. I was so relieved, so happy . . . I could feel tears stinging. So mad. Why would Jessica sneak away from our party and then go home and sneak up to her room? Didn't she think people would worry about her?

I hung up the phone, trying to push back the truth. When she had left my party, I had been too glad to be worried.

"Boy, is *that* a relief," said Lindsay. She ripped open a bag of corn curls and grabbed a handful. "I was getting so worried, I thought I was going to throw up."

"Why is Jessica acting this way?" I shook my

head to the offered corn curls. I was too upset to eat. "Poor Aunt Sharon. First Uncle Bernie is mean to her, and then her own daughter treats her this way."

Lindsay got up and poured herself some soda. "Maybe Jessica should go back to that doctor. 'Cause I remember this movie once, where this lady was real normal one day, and then she started getting weirder and weirder and she would never go to the doctor's, and finally she started eating wild squirrels."

My eyes crossed. "So, what are you trying to say, Lindsay?"

Lindsay shrugged. "That maybe Jessica is too weird for us to handle. MaryBeth doesn't even want her at her party."

"Her doctor said she would talk in a couple of weeks," I mentioned. Me thinking Jessica was weird was bad enough, but it sounded a lot more serious to have other people say it, too.

"But, that was before Jessica started running away," pointed out Lindsay. "I'll bet this will make the doctor write a whole lot more on her chart. Like, mute and . . . and dangerous runaway person. Last seen talking to a duck in Utah."

"You're crazy."

Lindsay grinned. "No, I'm not crazy, *Jessica's* crazy."

I didn't feel like smiling back. And even though my head hurt as if it were ready to split at the seams, I didn't want to give up on Jessica. I knew if she ever left Sweetwater, she wouldn't be coming back.

15

The next morning at breakfast, my dad insisted on making me French toast. A peace (piece) offering. Ha-ha.

"So, let's all go to church at ten o'clock, and then go over to Uncle Beau's and ride horses," suggested my dad.

"Oh, gosh, Wayne. I promised Sharon I'd take her to the new mall." My mother smiled at me. "Want to come, Callie? It would give you and Jessica some time together."

I kept chewing. After last night, I thought Jessica and I should have some time apart. Besides, I didn't want to be walking around the mall with Silent Sam.

"That sounds like a great idea," said my dad. He poured me a large glass of juice. "You're a good influence on her, Callie. The more time you can spend with her, the better."

I swallowed a large chunk of French toast and started to cough. "Better for who?"

"Whom," my mother corrected.

"Dad, I have tried and tried with Jessica. If the doctors in Pittsburgh can't make her talk, why do you think I can?" I stabbed another piece of toast, and then let the fork lie on my plate. I was losing my appetite.

"What harm can an hour at the mall do?" my mother wanted to know.

I shrugged. Probably give me a headache.

"Invite Lindsay, too," suggested my dad. "She talks non-stop."

"I'll see." I got up and rinsed my plate. The sun was shining and it would have been a great day for horseback riding. I wasn't Jessica's hired guardian. If I wanted to go riding with my dad, I should be allowed to do that.

"Maybe I'll stay home and paint the garage," my dad said cheerfully. "We can go riding next weekend."

I spun around at the sink. "But, I was thinking that maybe I would like to go riding with you, Dad. Just the two of us, like old times."

My dad winked. "Thanks, little girl. But next weekend might be even better. We can give Uncle Beau a little notice and let him arrange a little barbecue for Aunt Sharon and Jessica."

My mother laughed. "Wayne, that's a wonderful idea. I'll call Beau this afternoon and suggest it. We can all bring something and they have that huge new patio. Sharon and Jessica haven't been out to their place since they've been back."

"It's a nice day for riding, today, Dad." I pulled back the kitchen curtain so he could see how clear the sky was. "It might be raining next weekend."

My mother stood up and peered outside. "Oh, don't even say that, honey. We don't want rain for the welcome home barbecue. Maybe you and Lindsay can be in charge of the games for all the cousins."

I nodded. Lindsay and I were *always* in charge of the cousins. I grinned. "Okay, but I want a pay increase."

My father pretended he was searching for his wallet. "I'll up you a buck an hour."

I giggled. "Thanks, Dad. You still owe us for the past three Christmas Eve parties."

My dad laughed. "I'm still waiting to hit oil out back, Callie. You keep that tab running, though."

"Gosh, look at the time," said my mother. "Let's get ready for church. I'll call Sharon and tell her we'll be by at twelve-thirty."

"But, Mom, I don't know if I want to go to the mall."

My dad laughed. "You *love* the mall, Callie. You and Lindsay know sales clerks by their first names. I was even thinking of putting an escalator in here so you would feel more at home."

"Ha-ha." My father is so corny.

My mother unplugged the coffee maker and rushed past me. "I'll be downstairs in twenty minutes for church. Callie, you should wear your new print sundress; it's going to be a scorcher today."

My dad cracked open his paper. "I'm ready. Hurry up, ladies. I'll clean up the kitchen in a minute."

"I'm glad the mall is air-conditioned." My mother laughed as she headed upstairs. "Call Lindsay, Callie. See if her mom wants to join us. It will be a party!"

A party? For who, I mean, whom? Going to the mall might be more fun if Mom handed me her charge cards. There was no chance of that. The only thing she was letting me be in charge of was Jessica.

16

As soon as I was dressed for church, I called up Lindsay. "Please come with me, Lins!"

"You have *got* to be kidding, Callie. There is no way I want to go to the mall with Jessica," Lindsay declared flatly. "My mom spent twenty minutes yelling at me last night. She said I wasn't protecting her enough. She practically said I caused Jessica to run away."

"What? We didn't do anything to upset Jessica. Not on purpose, anyway."

"Yeah, exactly. I finally told my mom the talking duck puppet was your idea," added Lindsay with a grin. "So, then she stopped yelling at me."

"Oh, thanks, Lindsay." I wrapped the telephone cord around my finger. When in doubt, blame Callie.

"Well, sorry, Callie, but after being yelled at for such a long time, I was worn out. Besides, my

80

mom loves you and you weren't there to get yelled at."

"Well, I'll forgive you if you come with us. Please, Lindsay?" I begged. "I'll treat you to a yogurt cone."

Lindsay giggled. "Oh, gee, Callie. That's an offer I can refuse."

"And a gyro, Lindsay. And a medium drink. Oh, come on. I don't want to be stuck with Jessica all afternoon." I glanced behind me and lowered my voice. "My mom is making me go. Being the oldest cousin is very demanding."

I could hear Lindsay yawning at the other end of the line. "So, just tell them no."

"I can't."

"Well, I can. I'm going over to the park this afternoon to watch the hot air balloon. Want to come? They're having lots of craft and food booths, too."

"Sunday in the park! I do want to go. They're giving free rides in the balloon today."

"That's right. And the newspaper and television people will be there, too. We might end up on the front page."

"Right where we belong!"

"Our public demands it!" Lindsay laughed. "Wear eye makeup today, Callie. You film so much older that way."

"Let's get going," my dad called from the garage. "We won't get a seat."

"Lindsay, listen, I have to go to church now. I'll ask my mom if I can stay home afterwards and go to the park with you. Wait for me, okay?"

"Okay. But, Callie, as much as I love your company, I won't love it if you get stuck with Jessie."

"What's that supposed to mean?"

Lindsay sighed loudly. "It means that if you have to take Jessie, maybe you should just go to the mall. All the kids from school will be at the park. Scott Randel will be at the park!" Lindsay lowered her voice. "Don't think I'm mean, Callie, but I really don't want to baby-sit her today. I'll be doing enough of that once school starts. At least you won't have her following you through the halls."

"Okay, I'll tell my mom . . ." I paused, not sure of what I would tell my mom.

"Callie!" My father stuck his head into the kitchen.

"Coming!" I said good-bye to Lindsay and hung up. With any luck, I'd find a way during church to get out of going to the mall with Jessica, so I could have some fun with Lindsay and my other friends. I knew it was Sunday, and people were supposed to be extra kind to each other, but after last night, I needed a break. If I had one day off from Jessica, I would be extra nice and attentive for the rest of the week. My dad wouldn't even have to pay me for doing the games with the cousins next Sunday at Uncle Beau's.

All I was asking for was a day off! Wasn't Sunday supposed to be a day of rest?

17

After church, my mom changed clothes and left for the mall with Aunt Sharon. I waved goodbye from the front porch and then sank back down in the swing, not sure if I had gotten my own way or not.

"Well, the park does sound fun," my mother had said. "I guess you should go there instead of the mall."

"Maybe I'll walk down later," my dad had said. He reached in his wallet and handed me ten dollars. "Feel free to give me back my change."

"What change?" I laughed. Boy, I couldn't believe how well this whole change of plan routine was working. I was not going to be walking through the mall beside silent Jessica. I was going to be having lots of fun in the park with Lindsay.

"Treat Lindsay and Jessie to a cone," my mother suggested.

"What?"

"Treat your cousins," my mother repeated. "And wear sun screen, it's — "

"Mom, I wasn't planning on taking Jessica. I'm going with Lindsay."

My parents both looked at each other, exchanging that puzzled, can-this-be-our-Callie-talking? look.

My dad glanced at his ten dollars, like he should take part of it back.

"But, Aunt Sharon already told Jessica you were going to the mall with her, and . . ." My mother sighed. "I hope she won't be too disappointed. It won't be as much fun without you, Callie."

"I'll have lots of fun at the park," I answered honestly. "And Jessica will have fun with you two. She won't mind."

"I can't force you," my mother said slowly, probably wondering if she could.

"Thanks, Mom," I said cheerfully. "I'll go change."

"Callie?" My mother had her hand on the phone. "I'd better call Sharon and let her know you've changed your mind."

I shrugged. "Okay."

"What should I say?" This was not like my mother. She always knew what to say. Jessica was making everyone confused.

"Tell her the truth, that I'm going to the park."

How hard could it be? Aunt Sharon couldn't possibly expect me to be in charge of her daughter twenty-four hours a day. I gripped the banister more tightly, tasting how bitter my selfish words sounded. I was only trying to be honest. I'd do something with her tomorrow. Invite her to the pool, maybe. All I wanted was a day off.

I walked up to my bedroom at the top of the stairs. With each step, listening to my mother's soft, disappointed voice, I could feel myself weakening.

Dad came in and sat down beside me. "Hey, I thought you were going to the park."

"I am. I'm going to pick up Lindsay in a few minutes."

He patted me on the knee and smiled. "Have fun, honey. I might see you down there later. Save me a bowl of chili."

"Dad?"

"Yes?"

"You don't think I'm being selfish, do you? I'll do something with Jessica tomorrow."

"That sounds fine, Callie."

My dad got up and stretched. "I'd better get started on the garage."

"But do you think I'm being a little selfish?"

My dad studied me, scratching his chin and thinking.

"No, not selfish."

I stood up. My dad did think I was being *something*. I could tell.

"What am I being then?" I wanted to know.

My dad smiled and headed back downstairs. "Have fun, Callie."

"Dad!" I followed him to the front door and searched his face. "Dad, what am I being? I don't want you to think I'm mean."

My dad smiled at me and shook his head. "You're not mean, honey."

"But what am I then?" I asked quietly.

"Young."

18

"Young?" Lindsay stared into my face. "What did your dad mean by that? Is it a rip?"

"No, I don't think so." My dad never tries to hurt my feelings.

Lindsay unwrapped a piece of gum and folded it into her mouth. She tossed me a piece of peppermint. "Okay, now. So you asked your dad if you were being mean," Lindsay chewed fast. "Let me work this gum a second, Callie. Okay, so he said you weren't mean, just young." Lindsay chewed for another minute. Then she smiled. "Oh, I know what he meant now."

I felt relieved. Lindsay was pretty good at figuring things out. "What?"

"He meant you're still kind of stupid."

"What?"

Lindsay grinned. "But, nice stupid."

"Oh, thanks." Being stupid could be a positive thing, I guess.

"It's just like this movie I saw once," began Lindsay.

I groaned and knocked my hip against Lindsay's. "I'm not in the mood, Lindsay. Really."

Lindsay giggled. "No, this is really going to help you understand, Callie. Trust me."

We were almost at the park, so I had no choice. I wanted to get this thing off my chest so I could enjoy myself.

"In this movie, some real old black-and-white kind of story, with the women wearing pearls and the men always riding on trains, anyway . . ." Lindsay swallowed. "There was this nice, but stupid, girl, who reminded me of you, Callie."

"Go on," I said, hoping it wouldn't take too long. I didn't want any of our friends listening to Lindsay's stupid theories on stupidity.

"So, this girl kept doing the wrong things, kind of stupid things, but she never made mistakes on purpose."

"She was just stupid," I added.

Lindsay smiled, glad I was following her. "Yeah, like she would cook a dinner for this poor old man, but since she didn't know how to cook so well, the old man got really sick and almost died. And then once she offered to weed this old lady's garden, but she ended up pulling out her prized flowers and left the weeds. That kind of stuff."

"Stupid stuff."

Lindsay nodded. "Exactly."

"So? What happened to this girl? The stupid girl who reminds you of me."

Lindsay shrugged. "I don't know. It was on real late and my mom made me go to bed."

"Lindsay!"

"But, the point is, this stupid girl was really kind and smart, just too young to do things the right way." Lindsay tossed her gum in the weeds by the road. "So, I bet your dad watched the same movie and understands that you are trying hard to do the right thing with Jessica, but you're too young to know the right thing."

"What does that mean?"

Lindsay waved to MaryBeth and some girls standing by the tennis courts. "It means that the smart thing for you to do would have been to take Jessica to the mall. But since you're young, and kind of stupid, you chose to come to the park with me."

"You're crazy," I said. My cheeks were starting to burn and I knew it wasn't from the heat. "My dad thinks I made the right choice today. He understands why I needed a day off."

Lindsay raised one eyebrow and shook her head. "Oh yeah? Well then, how come he called you young?"

"Because I am young," I admitted. "And you

are, too, Lindsay. In fact, you're *younger* than I am."

Lindsay's eyes grew wide and she tossed her ponytail back with an angry flip. "Well, thank you very much, Callie."

"I just said you were young." I tried not to smile. This had to be the dumbest conversation I had ever had with Lindsay.

Lindsay grabbed my arm. "Oh, let's forget it. Come on, I want to tell MaryBeth I can come to her party. My mom said I could stay until ten."

"Race you," I shouted as I took off. Just then six hot air balloons were set free, floating up into the clear afternoon sky. My own heart felt lighter, too, as if the balloons had been a sign. Things were working out exactly the way they were supposed to work out. Nothing was going to spoil my day off.

19

By two o'clock Lindsay and I were both sunburned. I was down to three dollars, and the line for the hot air balloon was a mile long. My day off was wearing me out.

"I told MaryBeth we would meet her for a snow cone at two-fifteen, by the community booth," said Lindsay. She reached into her pocket and counted her money. "I only have fifty cents left. Will you loan me some money, Callie? I'll pay you back someday, I promise."

I handed her a dollar. "Maybe we should go home after this, Lindsay. My face is bright red."

Lindsay giggled. "Now it finally matches your hair."

"Want to walk back to my house and see if you can stay for dinner?"

Lindsay was walking on her tiptoes, searching the crowd. "Sure. I can't see Scott anywhere. I'll bet those television people spotted him and offered him his own show already."

"Do you see MaryBeth?"

"Oh, my gosh!" Lindsay grabbed both of my hands and pulled me into an alley between the hot pretzel booth and the information tent. "I do not believe it. I do not believe what I just saw. Oh, my gosh, Callie, we've got to hide!"

I wrestled my hands free. "What are you talking about?"

Lindsay took a few steps out and peered up and down the aisle. "She's coming closer." Lindsay pulled me further into the alley. "Does this park have a back door?"

"Lindsay, what are you talking about? Who's coming?"

"Zombie woman," Lindsay covered her mouth with her hand. "Ooops, sorry. I mean Jessica."

"Jessica? What is she doing here?" My mother must have told her about the park. Why would shy Jessica walk all over by herself? Why wasn't she at the mall?

Maybe she was looking for me, to thank me in person for deserting her.

"There you two are!"

"Yikes!" squealed Lindsay, squeezing her eyes tight.

"Hi, MaryBeth!" I tried to sound casual, like Lindsay and I always relaxed this way, crouched in an alley.

"What are you two doing?" laughed MaryBeth. "Is someone after you?"

Lindsay hopped up and smiled. "No, we were just resting, that's all. It's so hot out there."

MaryBeth rolled her eyes. "It's a lot cooler than in here. It's like an oven."

As if on cue, a bead of sweat rolled down the center of my back.

"Yeah, but you know what I always say," laughed Lindsay. "Nothing like sweat to get the bad blood out."

"What?" MaryBeth made a face. "Lindsay, you are *so* strange at times."

Lindsay looked insulted, then worried. "Well, actually, I never said that. A girl in a circus movie said it. She was afraid to get tattooed, 'cause the guy with the electric needle could only see out of one eye, and — "

"Let's get those snow cones," I said quickly. I grabbed MaryBeth's arm and pulled her back into the sunlight.

As soon as my eyes adjusted to the bright light, I shut them and groaned. There was Jessica, three feet from me, wearing a Pittsburgh Pirates T-shirt and the meanest look on her face.

"Oh, hi," MaryBeth said weakly. "How are you, Jessica?"

Jessica shrugged, craning her neck forward to shoot Lindsay a dirty look. Why was she so mad at us, anyway? It wasn't as if this park festival was a private party organized by us.

"Jessica, hi," said Lindsay. She pinched my

back. "We were going to get a snow cone. Want one?"

Jessica shook her head, then started walking. She passed all three of us and never once looked back.

"Well, that was in-ter-es-ting," whispered MaryBeth. "What is she so mad about?"

"Nothing," I said. My heart was acting up again, practically shouting, tilt, tilt! Why did I feel so guilty? What was I supposed to do now? Run after her? Beg her to walk around with Lindsay, MaryBeth, and me?

"Jessica isn't mad," said Lindsay. She elbowed MaryBeth. "This is kind of confidential, but I can tell you. I mean, since I'm coming to your party and everything."

"Lindsay," I warned. I wasn't sure of what she was going to say, but I was pretty sure it would be the wrong thing.

Lindsay grinned at me and waved me away with her hand. "Oh, don't worry, Callie. I'm not going to tell her about Jessica running away last night. I just want MaryBeth to know that the psychologist thinks Jessica will snap out of this. He said she should start talking again soon."

MaryBeth's eyes opened wide. "Psychologist? Aren't they doctors that you go to when you're nuts?"

"No," I said quickly.

Lindsay laughed. "No, that's a psychiatrist.

Jessica is just starting out. You start out with psychologists. Then, if they can't fix you, you go to — "

"Be quiet, Lindsay!" I reached out and gave her a push. "Honestly, Lindsay. Don't you know when to keep your mouth shut?"

Lindsay held out both hands. "Hey, what did I say?"

MaryBeth shook her head. "I don't know, guys. This sounds pretty serious. I thought your cousin was just a little shy, but . . ."

"Jessica is okay." I glared at Lindsay, wishing I had my snow cone now so I could throw it at her. MaryBeth was a nice girl, but she had tons of friends, and if she told even half of them, the whole town would know that something was wrong with Jessica.

"Well, it's not like Jessica is ready to audition for *Psycho III*," said Lindsay. "I mean, I wouldn't be afraid to take a shower or anything like that — "

"Be quiet, Lindsay! You are so . . . so . . . *YOUNG!*" I guess I was pretty loud, because MaryBeth jumped, Lindsay burst into tears, and Jessica, way up by the balloon stand, stared bullets at me.

20

"**E**veryone just calm down," I ordered.

"Don't tell me what to do," sniffed Lindsay. "Besides, since I'm so *YOOOOOOOUNG*, I probably can't understand you."

MaryBeth grinned, then started to laugh. "You guys are so weird! I guess I'm lucky that my only cousin is eight months old."

Lindsay nodded her head. "You are lucky, MaryBeth. I'm going to call one of those lawyer numbers on television and see if I can disown Callie and Jessica."

MaryBeth snickered. "See if you can do it before my party, okay? I don't want you two fighting. It really ruins the mood of a party."

"Fine," said Lindsay. She glared at me.

"Fine," I agreed. "In fact, maybe both of us shouldn't come, MaryBeth." I knew that was a mean trick, because of course MaryBeth would choose me, since we were the same age and she had been my friend first.

MaryBeth chewed on her lip. "Maybe that would be a good idea."

"It's a stupid idea!" snapped Lindsay. When she saw how startled MaryBeth looked, she tried to laugh. "I mean, Callie and I are great friends."

"Sure," I said. "At least we were."

Lindsay narrowed her eyes. "We still are, Callie."

MaryBeth held up both hands. "Listen, I've got to go. You guys decide. I don't care who comes, as long as the fighting doesn't come."

"That sounds fair. I won't fight with Lindsay if she remembers not to call Jessica a zombie." I glanced at Jessica, standing by herself, watching us.

"I don't want to get you mad, Callie," laughed MaryBeth. "But Jessica does act like a zombie. I mean, she never says a word. She just stares and stares. It gives me the creeps."

"You never know what creepy thing Jessica is going to do next," said Lindsay. She slapped her hand over her mouth and looked at me. "Sorry, Callie."

"See you later." MaryBeth walked across the park to the bike stand.

"Whoa, that was close," said Lindsay. "I thought she was going to uninvite both of us."

"Who cares?" I said. "MaryBeth can't tell us what to do. Maybe we should bring Jessie to her party, just to show her we can think for ourselves."

"Callie, I don't want to think for myself right now," wailed Lindsay. "I just want to go to MaryBeth's party. And Jessica won't even find out that we went. I mean, she isn't talking to anyone and — "

"Don't call her a zombie again or I'll slug you," I warned.

Lindsay frowned. "You'd actually slug me? Oh, that's great, Callie. I'm going home."

"Good."

"Fine."

Lindsay marched off, giving Jessica a brief wave as she passed her.

I glanced at my watch. Two-thirty. My day off was over. Time to get back to work.

"Jessica, wait up!" I ran across the grass and caught up with her. "Hi. Having fun?"

Jessica nodded, then shook her head. She looked pretty miserable.

"Lindsay and I had a fight," I confided. "I guess you heard us yelling." Since Jessica didn't talk, I knew she wouldn't ask me what the fight had been about. "Boy, that girl says some stupid things sometimes."

Jessica just stared at me. She looked a little surprised that I was saying something mean about Lindsay.

"It's okay, Jessica," I said. "I love Lindsay, but she drives me nuts sometimes. She doesn't know when to keep her mouth shut." I laughed. "And you don't know when to open yours. Ha, pretty funny, huh?"

Jessica stopped and handed the snow cone lady a dollar. She waited and got her blue snow cone and change.

"Oh, that looks good," I said cheerfully. "I'll take one, too."

"There you go," said the lady. "Have a nice day now."

I looked over at Jessica, wondering if she realized the lady hadn't said a word to her.

What would happen once Jessica started school? What if the kids, and finally the teachers, stopped talking to her? What if Jessica ended up stuck in the sixth grade without any friends at all?

"Jessica, I know you're upset, but when do you think you'll start talking? I mean, no offense, but some of the kids think you're weird."

Jessica turned, her mouth hanging open, shocked. I could see her bright blue tongue.

"You probably stopped talking because your dad left you guys, but . . ."

Jessica started walking faster.

"Jessica, don't get mad at me. I mean, everyone is getting mad at me lately because they all think I know how to help you. But, I don't."

Jessica let her snow cone fall from her hand.

She turned toward the parking lot, walking faster than ever.

"Wait a minute." I reached out and grabbed Jessica's arm. "Stop running away. I want to help you, Jessica. I know you must feel awful inside. But *we* didn't do anything to you. Why are you so mad at us? What did I do to you?"

Jessica twisted away from me.

"Be mad at your dad if you want to be mad at someone," I snapped. "It's all *his* fault. He's gone. He doesn't even know you stopped talking to everyone. He doesn't even care, Jessica. We care; your mom cares!" I could see tears welling up in her eyes. She lowered her head and turned away.

"At least start talking to your mom," I said softly. "She loves you."

Jessica shook her head.

"You can talk to me," I said. "I promise to listen."

Jessica looked up, and for one brief second I thought she was going to speak. In fact, I had no idea she was even mad, until she slapped me.

21

I stayed away from Lindsay and Jessica for the next few days. I helped my dad finish painting the garage, went antiquing with my mom, and even baby-sat for a lady with four kids. It was busy work, but a lot *less* work than protecting Jessica or arguing with Lindsay.

My mom started to worry about me on Friday afternoon when I offered to help her with the laundry. "Callie, you've been hanging around the house all week. Why don't you call Lindsay or MaryBeth and go swimming? It's going to be eighty-five today."

I picked up two of my dad's dark socks and knotted them. "I like being with you, Mom. Want to play cards after we finish the wash?"

My mother laughed. "Go call Lindsay! I miss her face around here."

"I don't." As soon as the words were out, I could hear how false they sounded. I missed Lindsay a lot. MaryBeth's party was a day away and I wasn't even sure I was going to go if I had to walk in without Lindsay.

My mother closed the lid of the washing machine and headed back upstairs. "I'm going to call Aunt Sharon, honey. Do you want to use the phone first? I might be a while."

I waited a beat, sure my mom was going to say, "Oh, by the way, why don't you ask Jessica to go swimming, too?" But my mom didn't. In fact, my mom hadn't asked me to do anything with Jessica for days. For five days, in fact!

Maybe she had heard about Jessica slapping me and wanted to protect me from her.

"Hey, Mom," I said, catching up with her in the kitchen. "Did you know Jessica went to the fair in the park last Sunday? After you left for the mall with Aunt Sharon?"

My mom's face flooded red. She bit her lip and looked as if I had caught her red-handed!

"Callie, I didn't want to mention it . . ."

"Did you know Jessica slapped me?"

My mother nodded. How could she have known and not said a word about it?

"Who told you?" Now that I knew I had been neglected, I wanted to know all the facts. "I don't even know why she slapped me." Well, actually, I had thought about it a lot since Sunday and I figured Jessica had slapped me because I had said her dad didn't care about her. That was mean of me. If I had a second chance, I would have said something else. Something that Jessica may have just nodded to, instead of slapping me in front of half the town.

"Aunt Sharon told me," said my mother.

"Who told Aunt Sharon?" How embarrassing if people were still talking about the cousins who fight in public.

"Jessica told her mother about it as soon as we got back from the mall."

"*Jessica?* You mean she talked?"

My mother smiled and looked worried all at the same time. "She talked a little on Sunday, and then a little on Monday and Tuesday. Not too much. But enough to encourage Sharon to contact a doctor down here so Jessica can talk to him about her feelings."

"Wow!" This was just like something out of Lindsay's old-time movies. "Can I call Jessica on the phone?"

My mother's face lost a little bit of its sparkle. "No, Callie. It's much too soon for that. Jessica still won't talk to everyone. I saw her yesterday and she only nodded again."

"Probably because you're related to me," I said miserably. "Jessica hates me, Mom."

"No, she doesn't." My mom put her arms around me and gave me a hug. "And I love you."

I hugged her back. "I insulted Uncle Bernie. That's why Jessica slapped me."

"Well, her slapping you helped a little," my mother said softly.

"It sure didn't help me," I said. "I felt like an idiot. I think Scott Randel saw the whole thing."

My mother patted my back and sighed. "Don't worry about Scott. Now why don't you call Lindsay and go have some fun?"

"Okay." I picked up the phone to call Lindsay and smiled. I couldn't believe we had stayed mad at each other this long. She would die when I told her about Jessica slapping me while Scott watched from the tennis courts. And wait till she heard about the peanut butter, marshmallow fluff, and Cheerio sandwich I had to fix all four kids when I baby-sat. In fact, I had sooooo much to tell Lindsay, we'd be talking non-stop all the way through MaryBeth's party tomorrow night.

22

On Saturday, before Lindsay came over, my mom surprised me with a new white tank top, embroidered with tiny red hearts. She said it was because I helped with painting the garage and laundry, but I think she just wanted to cheer me up. Whenever I thought nobody was looking, I worried about Jessica. As much as I tried to forget about her problems, I couldn't. Worse yet, I could barely understand them. I couldn't even imagine my dad being mean to Mom and me.

A few hours later, Lindsay was leaning across the sink and brushing on some blusher. I'd bought it at Woolworth's last summer, but this was the first time I had unwrapped the cellophane.

"You look so nice, Callie. You finally have a suntan," said Lindsay. "And, thanks to this blusher, no one would know you had been slapped on that cheek."

"Lindsay!" I flicked my wet toothbrush at her.

"Don't tell anyone about me being slapped. I mean it."

"Okay, okay, you made your point, lady." Lindsay leaned back against my mirror. All of a sudden she looked sad.

"Lindsay, I'm not trying to boss you around again, but I don't think we should talk about the weird stuff Jessica does. Now that she's seeing another doctor, she might get better real fast. Won't that be great?"

Lindsay nodded, then lowered her head and started picking at her nails.

"What's wrong?"

"Nothing."

I tossed my toothbrush aside and hopped up beside her on my bathroom vanity. "I know you're trying to let your nails grow and you're a second away from ripping them all off, so what's bugging you?"

Lindsay blinked and a solitary tear rolled down her cheek.

"Lindsay, what's wrong?" I was so used to my cousin being funny and carefree all the time, it was strange to see her unhappy.

"I'm real glad that Jessica is going to get better," Lindsay said, "but what if . . ." Lindsay stopped and wiped her cheeks dry. "What if you two start to be best friends. Like *we're* best friends? What if you forget about me?"

"That's stupid!" I said, reaching out and patting her knee.

"It happens," Lindsay whispered. "I saw this movie once, and — "

"Lindsay," I warned.

"Well, excuse me if I'm the only one who knows that old movies are so smart. I want us to be best friends even when we're old and get married and have little kids and clip coupons, and — "

"You'll always be my best friend, Lindsay." I hopped off the sink before I started crying, too. "Come on, let's go down and see if my parents saved us any pizza."

I gave Lindsay a cold rag for her splotchy face and we both went downstairs. My parents were going over to a neighbor's for dessert and Lindsay and I were on our own as far as walking to MaryBeth's house for the party at seven o'clock. My dad said he would be over at ten to pick us up.

"Oh, yippeee!" I said, peering into the pizza box. "They saved us six pieces."

"Gross," groaned Lindsay. "Whenever I cry, I can't eat. I'll take two pieces."

I laughed and popped four pieces into the microwave. "You eat like a bird, Lindsay."

"Yeah, well, I *look* like a mess."

"You look pretty." I brushed back her blonde hair. "Want me to redo your ponytail?"

"Won't do any good." Lindsay slid her chin into

her hand. "I don't think I'll ever be glamorous, Callie. I think I'll look like this, forever."

I laughed. "You're not even old enough for braces. How can you know?"

Lindsay shook back her hair. "That's the scary part, Callie. Sometimes you don't know anything until it's already happened."

"What?"

Lindsay sat up straighter, as if she had finally found some direction. "Last summer Uncle Beau took me and my mom to a movie."

Since Lindsay was already upset, I tried not to groan.

"And this girl in the movie was born after her parents had been shipwrecked on this island. So the poor kid had no idea that there were cities with a million or billion people living there." Lindsay looked over at me for encouragement. I shot her back my best I-can-hardly-wait-for-the-ending look.

"So, once they were rescued, this girl was real surprised to know that not everyone liked coconuts for breakfast and that some people had different skin and hair colors, and that some could sing and play the piano. Things that were different from this girl."

"Yeah, so?"

"So." Lindsay sucked in a deep breath. "So, then this girl had to realize that even though she was somebody special to her parents on the island, when she was rescued, she was just kind of . . . well, regular, and not so special."

I couldn't help it: I groaned.

"You've lost me, Lindsay. What are you trying to say?"

Lindsay put down her pizza and started pacing around the kitchen. "I'm saying that I'm just *real* average. Nothing special. Maybe you hang around with me because I'm the cousin closest to you in age. But, what if you decide that Jessica is the *best* cousin? She can draw and do gymnastics. Things I can't do. So, what if you think she's more fun than me, then what? What about me?"

"Lindsay!" I felt so bad about her being upset. And it was for nothing. "No one in the world could take your place, Lindsay. Now eat your pizza. We still have to finish getting ready for MaryBeth's party."

"MaryBeth said that her mom is going to make homemade ice cream and . . . Yikkkesss!" Lindsay grabbed me and pushed me in front of her like a shield. "Jessica, what are you doing here? I mean, so, hi, how are you?" Lindsay gushed. Her nails were digging into my brand-new tank top.

"Hi, Jessie. Want some pizza?" I asked. I felt a little nervous, not because I was afraid Jessica was going to slap me again, but because I was pretty sure one of us should start things off by saying, "I'm sorry." Which one should go first?

Jessica shook her head and walked into the

kitchen, laying a huge picture album on the kitchen table.

"Whoa, that's a *huge* album," cried Lindsay. She released her grip on me and dove for the album, flipping through the pages. "Oh, my gosh, look how little we were. Oh, Callie, look at this picture. You didn't have any front teeth; how cute!"

"Where?" I couldn't remember not having teeth. Maybe Jessica had blackened them out with a marker on Sunday after I insulted her dad.

I slid into the chair next to Lindsay. "Hey, look at this. I don't remember all three of us riding Uncle Beau's white horse. He never lets anyone get on that mare."

"It was my birthday."

Chills raced up my clammy arms. It had been so long since I had heard Jessica say a whole sentence, I thought I was going to cry and cheer all at the same time. But I bit my tongue instead. I didn't want to scare her off.

"You're *talking*," cried Lindsay. She hopped up from her chair and threw her arms around her. "Oh, Jessie, this is great. This is just like the movie, *Heidi*, when Clara gets out of the wheelchair and walks to her dad and — "

"Lindsay!" I tried to pry her off Jessica, but then I noticed that Jessica was hugging her back.

"You're nuts," Jessica said softly. But she was smiling.

I felt like an outsider, watching them hug. But since Jessica had slapped me a few days before, I didn't want to rush right in and grab her.

"This is great, just great," sighed Lindsay, sinking back into her chair and picking up the album. "Oh, look at the twins. They seem cuter when they're in a picture."

Jessica pulled out a chair and sat down.

"Callie and I were going to bring an album over to you, too," began Lindsay cheerfully. "But, we never got around to getting all the pictures together. We have ten half-filled albums all over the house. You're lucky your mom is so organized. I can't believe you have so many pictures of the three of us. Boy, were we adorable!" Lindsay held up one hand. "Correction, ladies, we *are* adorable! Thank your mom for us."

"I did it," said Jessica.

"You did?" I was impressed. There were dozens of pictures, with dates and holidays marked with neat little signs.

"Here we are at Granddaddy's for Christmas," laughed Lindsay. She looked closer at the picture. "Hey, this isn't so hot of me. Why am I crying?"

I studied the picture. "Maybe you got coal for Christmas."

Lindsay made a face at me. Then she pushed the album in front of Jessica. "Why was I crying?"

"The twins tried to feed your new doll some cranberry sauce."

"That's *right*! I remember now. That poor doll still has a smeared-up face," cried Lindsay. "Boy, those boys are trouble."

In the living room, the grandfather clock chimed seven.

"Oops, we're going to be late." Lindsay stood up and closed the album. She glanced at Jessica and slapped her hand over her mouth. "I mean . . ."

Jessica stood up quickly. " 'Bye."

"Wait a minute," I said quickly. "You don't have to go, Jessica."

Jessica looked over at Lindsay.

Lindsay's face grew pink. "Sorry, Jessica. MaryBeth is having a party. A small party. But, we don't have to go."

Jessica turned to leave.

"Neither one of us wants to go now," I said. "It would be a lot more fun if you stayed and we looked at the album."

"Well." Jessica shrugged.

"And, I'm sorry, Jessica," I stammered. "About the stupid things I said in the park."

"I'm sorry, too, Callie," Jessica said softly.

"Want to stay?" I asked again. MaryBeth wouldn't miss us too much.

Lindsay clapped her hands and grinned.

"Please, Jessie? Just like old times."

Jessica agreed right away. "Sure. Sounds fun."

Lindsay walked over and linked arms with Jessica and me. "Ladies, do you know why this is so great?"

"Lindsay," I warned. I could feel it coming.

Jessica started to giggle.

"No, wait, listen," laughed Lindsay. "This will only take a second. It was a very *short* movie . . ."

"Lindsay," I said, holding up one hand. "At least let me make some popcorn, first."

"I'll get the butter," offered Lindsay.

"I'll get the big blue bowl," laughed Jessica. She walked over to the pantry and pulled it from the top shelf where my mother always kept it.

"Pretty good memory, Jessica." Lindsay tossed her a stick of butter. "You remember everything."

Jessica smiled. "Who could forget you two?"

"You mean, we three!" I added.

"No one, dar-ling," said Lindsay.

I smiled over at them both. "Who would even try?"

About the Author

Colleen O'Shaughnessy McKenna began her writing career as a child, when she sent off a script for the *Bonanza* series. McKenna is best known for her popular Murphy series, the inspiration for which comes from her own family.

A former elementary school teacher, Ms. McKenna lives in Pittsburgh, Pennsylvania, with her husband and four children.

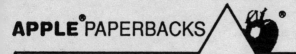